A moment passed and neither made any effort to move, still gazing at each other, memorizing each fine line that detailed their expressions.

Collin's eyes flickered closed and then open. "I swear," he repeated. "I'm going."

She laughed, acutely aware of the urgent matter pressing tightly against the front of his slacks for attention. She shifted her body forward until she was pressed firmly against him. His arm tightened around her waist, his fingers gripping the back of her dress.

"You're not playing fair," he said. "You know what you're doing to me, right?" He pushed his pelvis forward, the gesture teasing.

"That feels like a personal problem to me."

"Oh, it's very personal. It's about as personal as you can get."

"I imagine that's why you haven't moved yet?"

"That, and you need to move first. Unless you want me to roll over you?"

London giggled softly. She pushed her body even closer against his.

"London," he started, "maybe we should…"

"Maybe we should just stop talking," she said. She trailed her fingertips along the profile of his face. "In fact, I can think of a few other things we could be doing," she concluded, and then she kissed him, capturing his luscious lips with her own.

Dear Reader,

When a man has dreams that revolve around a woman he loves, he knows everything is possible and there is nothing that's insurmountable. Baby boy Collin Stallion is all grown up, and his days of stealing cars are long behind him. He's standing on the right side of the law, and the only thing he's stealing now is a woman's heart. London Jacobs talks a great game, and the only rules she plays by are the ones she sets. But there is something about Collin that has her breaking those rules like there's no tomorrow. He's the game changer that has her fantasizing about her own big dreams!

This Stallion son hasn't fallen far from the family tree and I absolutely adore him. Collin makes my heart sing, and I hope you'll enjoy his journey toward love as much as I enjoyed writing it. Together, Collin and London are sheer joy!

Thank you so much for your support. This is my last Kimani title, and my success with the Stallion and Boudreaux families would not have been possible without all of you. I am humbled by all the love you continue to show me, my characters and our stories. I can't begin to express how grateful I am.

Until the next series and the next family and definitely the next story, please take care, and may God's blessings be with you always.

With much love,

Deborah Fletcher Mello

www.DeborahMello.Blogspot.com

$\mathcal{A}$ $\mathcal{S}$tallion DREAM

DEBORAH FLETCHER MELLO

HARLEQUIN® KIMANI™ ROMANCE

Recycling programs
for this product may
not exist in your area.

ISBN-13: 978-1-335-21682-3

A Stallion Dream

Printed in U.S.A.

HARLEQUIN®
www.Harlequin.com

A12006 874189

Writing since forever, **Deborah Fletcher Mello** can't imagine herself doing anything else. Her first novel, *Take Me to Heart*, earned her a 2004 Romance Slam Jam nomination for Best New Author. In 2008, Deborah won the RT Reviewers' Choice award for Best Series Romance for her ninth novel, *Tame a Wild Stallion*. Deborah received a BRAB 2015 Reading Warrior Award for Best Series for her Stallion family series. Deborah was also named the 2016 Romance Slam Jam Author of the Year. She has also received accolades from several publications, including *Publishers Weekly*, *Library Journal* and *RT Book Reviews*. With each new book, Deborah continues to create unique story lines and memorable characters. Born and raised in Connecticut, Deborah now considers home to be wherever the moment moves her.

Books by Deborah Fletcher Mello

Harlequin Kimani Romance

Truly Yours
Hearts Afire
Twelve Days of Pleasure
My Stallion Heart
Stallion Magic
Tuscan Heat
A Stallion's Touch
A Pleasing Temptation
Sweet Stallion
To Tempt a Stallion
A Stallion Dream

Visit the Author Profile page
at Harlequin.com for more titles.

To Nanette Kelley!
You have renewed my faith!
I can play in the sandbox again, and
I am grateful that you are there
to share in the joy with me!
I love you to pieces!

Chapter 1

"Collin! Collin! Hey, Collin!"

Collin Stallion winced as his little brother—Matthew Jacoby Stallion Junior, affectionately known as Jake—screamed for his attention. His younger sibling was somewhere on the other side of the family home, his high-pitched squeal sounding like fingernails grating against a chalkboard. Collin had only been back for a few short hours and the ten-year old had been screaming his name every few minutes like clockwork. He'd screamed for Collin to come see his new Black Panther toys. He'd screamed for Collin to come play video games on his Xbox system. He'd screamed for Collin every time his big brother managed to get out of his sight. Jake screaming his name had begun to wear on his big brother's nerves.

Their mother moved into the room, swiping her

hands on a dish towel. Katrina Stallion laughed warmly, "He missed you, Collin. Cut him some slack."

"I know, Mom, but I'm going to be here for a minute. Do we really have to catch up on everything in one day?"

Collin's mother laughed again, "Your little brother is ecstatic to have you home. He idolizes you. So, please, don't you give him a hard time. By tomorrow he'll be back to his regular routine and isn't going to care about you being around until you get ready to leave again."

Before Collin could respond, Jake came bounding into the room, still yelling out his brother's name. "Collin!"

Collin took a deep breath and held it for a brief second before he answered. "Yes, Jake? What's up, buddy?" He dropped the book he'd been reading to his lap.

"There's a man at the door for you."

"For me?"

Jake nodded. "He says it's important. He has a delivery for you."

Collin shot his mother a look, puzzlement shifting between them. Katrina shrugged her narrow shoulders, having no answers about who was seeking him out or what they wanted. Collin slid his book onto the coffee table and stood up.

Jake grabbed his hand and tugged. "Come on," he chided, a silly grin widening across his face. The youngster pulled his brother through the family home to the foyer and the front door.

A well-dressed man wearing tan linen slacks and

a white dress shirt smiled in greeting. "Good afternoon, sir. Are you Collin Stallion?"

"Yes, I am. How may I help you?"

"I just need to confirm your identification and then get your signature, Mr. Stallion," the man said as he extended a metal clipboard in Collin's direction.

Collin scanned the documents attached, noting a delivery receipt that required his signature to acknowledge his acceptance. "I'm sorry, but what is this for?" he asked.

The man took a step back and gestured over his shoulder. Sitting in the driveway of the Sunnybrook Lane property, directly in front of the four-car garage, was a black-on-black Mercedes C-300 sedan with a huge red bow adorning the hood. The brand-new vehicle was gleaming under the midday sun, looking like it had been spit-polished with multiple coats of car wax. The windows were tinted, and new sports rims adorned the frame.

"There's a card," the man said, gesturing to the paperwork in Collin's hand. "But I do need your signature first, sir!"

Still puzzled, Collin read through the fine print quickly, then scribbled his moniker across the dotted line. He handed the clipboard back. The deliveryman snatched a duplicate copy from the bottom of the document and passed it and an envelope to Collin. He reached into his pocket for a set of keys and passed them to him, as well. "Congratulations," he said as he did an about-face and stepped down off the porch.

Collin stepped out of the house after the man. He watched as the stranger slid into the passenger seat of the Mercedes dealership's service van, the vehicle eventually pulling out of the driveway and disappearing into midday traffic.

"It's so cool!" Jake exclaimed as he bounded down the steps and peered into the driver's-side window. "Who gave you a car?"

"I want to know who it's from, too! Are you going to open your card?" Katrina asked.

Collin turned to find his mother, and his father, standing behind him. Still stunned by the delivery, he stood like a deer in headlights, uncertain and slightly lost.

Matthew Stallion shot his wife a look. "Is he okay?"

She laughed, "I'm not sure."

Collin shook his head. His eyes were blinking rapidly. "I'm just... It's... W-well..." he stammered and then he noticed his hand was shaking.

Matthew laughed, "I think our son needs some help."

Katrina reached for the envelope and pulled it from Collin's palm. She took the note card from inside and gave her son a questioning glance, and he nodded his approval for her to read it aloud.

His mother read it to herself first, drawing her hand to her heart as tears suddenly misted her eyes. She exchanged a look with her husband, who rested a gentle hand against the small of her back. She nodded her head slightly and then began to read.

"'Collin, you were fifteen when I promised you that if you did what was asked of you and followed the rules, you, too, could have your own Mercedes. You've earned this. Your mother and I could not be prouder. We love you very much! Congratulations, son! Dad. PS Try not to get it stolen!'"

"Thank you!" Collin exclaimed, his excitement spilling past his eyes. He moved into his father's arms, the two men embracing warmly.

Matthew grinned. "I'm proud of you, son," he said as he slapped Collin across the back. "Now, go check out your car," he said. "Maybe take your little brother for a ride!"

Collin swiped a hand over his eyes as he leaned to kiss his mother's cheek. "I love you," he said and then took the porch steps two at a time, eager to explore his new vehicle.

Collin listened with half an ear as Jake rambled on about *Star Wars*, the newest Avengers movie and some little girl named Melissa, who kept giving him cookies at lunchtime. The two had been riding around for hours, finally stopping at In-N-Out Burger when Jake complained about being hungry. He was finishing off the last of his double-double burger and fries as he filled his brother in on everything that was important to him in his small world.

Collin had forgotten what it was like to be his brother's age—not having a care in the world and still feeling like the weight of everything rested on your shoulders. He had been a sixteen-year-old with his own problems when Jake had been born. His saving grace had been their father.

Collin had been fifteen years old when he first met Matthew Stallion in family court. He'd been facing criminal charges for stealing Matthew's car. He hadn't been thinking when he'd swiped the luxury Mercedes for a joyride. After crashing it on the interstate he'd been given probation and an opportunity to change his circumstances around. Matthew had become his mentor, and then his mother's husband. For the first time in his life, Collin had a father who was there to greet him each morning and wish him good-night every evening. Matthew had stepped up to be his parent, taking the place of his biological father, who had died in military service when Collin had been a baby. On his eighteenth birthday, Matthew had asked to legally adopt him, wanting to give Collin his name. That moment had been the happiest in his young life and the framed photo of them back in family court was one he cherished.

Collin had fond memories of their father listening intently as he whined about problems that weren't problems, and he wanted his baby brother to know the same joy. Even though he knew there were times his dad had only been listening with half an ear, his thoughts also on business and issues that didn't concern his sons, Matthew had never let him see that he wasn't the most important thing in that moment.

Jake beamed up at him. "I hope Dad buys me a car when I graduate from law school."

"Just do what you're told, follow the rules, and I'm sure you'll get one, too, someday."

"I want a BMW, though. Or maybe a Tesla."

Collin laughed, "You have expensive taste."

"Says the guy who just got a free Mercedes!" Jake grinned, his wide smile like a beacon in the center of his small face. He took a sip of his soda, sucking the beverage loudly through his straw.

"We need to get back," Collin said as he reached for a paper napkin to wipe his hands. "Mom's going to be mad that we ate when she was planning to cook dinner."

"I'll be hungry again by the time we get back. It won't go to waste."

Collin laughed. Jake continued to talk, barely stopping to catch his breath. He had missed Collin and it showed in the young boy's exuberance. Collin let his brother ramble, feigning interest in stories about superheroes and girls who smelled like bubble gum. An hour later, when he pulled his new car back into the driveway of their home, Jake was past ready to go back to his video games and give his big brother some very welcome space.

"That boy is out like a light," Matthew said as he returned to the dining room table. "What did you do to him?" he asked, his eyes locking on Collin.

Collin shrugged. "I didn't do anything."

"He didn't sleep last night. He was so excited, and he was up at the crack of dawn. He needs to rest. And you, Mr. Stallion, need to get your foot trunk out of my SUV and take it to your room so you can unpack," Katrina admonished.

"Yes, ma'am."

She leaned to kiss the top of her son's head. "So, we redid the guest suite. Your father and I thought you might like a little more privacy until you figure out your plans. You'll have your own entrance with your own key. The fridge and pantry are fully stocked, so if you want to make your own meals you can, but you are always welcome to eat with us."

"I still grill on Fridays and Saturdays," Matthew

said, "so you're guaranteed a good meal at least two days out of the week." He winked at Collin.

"I know you are not talking badly about my cooking," Katrina said as she moved to her husband's side. She wrapped her arms around his broad shoulders and leaned to kiss his lips.

"Not at all. I was just reminding our son that we eat steaks on Friday."

"And Saturday," Collin said with a wide grin across his face. He held up two fingers. "Two! Two days of good food!"

"You two think you're funny!" Katrina said, giggling softly. "I'm done with the both of you."

"Family breakfast is the same time tomorrow?" Collin asked.

His mother nodded. "Food will be on the table at nine o'clock sharp. And we're all going to church at eleven. We have much to be thankful for and I'm thinking you could use a little prayer to kick off your week."

"Yes, ma'am."

"We also need to talk about you getting a haircut," Katrina said. She pulled her fingers through the length of his dreadlocks. "Something a little more befitting of the courtroom." Her eyes were wide as she looked from her son to her husband, and back.

"I'm not cutting my hair, Mom," Collin said, his tone firm.

Katrina crossed her arms over her chest. "Matthew, please talk to your son!"

"So, now he's my son because he doesn't want to cut his hair?"

"Support me here, please!"

Matthew shook his head. "Darling, I love you. But we are not going to win this argument. You've been trying since he graduated high school and decided to lock his hair. It's time to let it go," he chuckled softly.

"Uncle Mark is one of the state's top attorneys and no one ever says anything about his dreadlocks."

"Oh, they say things," Katrina muttered under her breath. She tossed her husband a look.

Matthew laughed heartily, "That's okay, baby. I know the ladies love my brother's rugged good looks and I've heard most of your friends say how they would love to run their hands through that full head of hair he has."

Katrina tossed the man another dry look. "You really are no help, Matthew Stallion."

Collin grinned. "I'll tell you what, Mom. I'll give it some consideration, but I can't promise you anything. The girls like to slide their fingers through my hair, too!"

Matthew and Collin both laughed heartily as Katrina threw her hands up in frustration. The two men watched as she made her exit, stopping to give them both one last kiss before retiring for the night.

Matthew stood and moved to the sideboard. He filled two glasses with scotch and passed one to Collin as he sat down with the other.

"You've impressed me, son. You've worked hard these past few years and I'm very proud of you. Graduating top of your class at Harvard, then finishing law school early and passing the state bar in Massachusetts and here in Texas on your first attempts. Those are quite the accomplishments."

A look crossed over Collin's face, giving Matthew

pause. His gaze narrowed ever so slightly as he stared at his eldest child. "Do you want to talk about it?"

"Sir?"

"What's bothering you, son? You haven't been yourself since you arrived. You've been quiet and withdrawn. So, why don't you tell me what's on your mind?"

Collin took a deep breath before answering. "After you finished law school, were you scared at all about what came next?"

Matthew took a slow sip of his cocktail before he responded. "I was. I wasn't sure I'd made the right decision. It took a while before I got my bearings and realized corporate law was what I really wanted to do."

"I'm not sure it's what I want, Dad. But I don't want to disappoint you."

Matthew shook his head. "You wouldn't disappoint me, son. You're an adult now. The choices you make for your life must be about what you want and what you need. You've done everything your mother and I have ever asked of you and in most cases, you excelled beyond our expectations. It's now your time and you need to make the most of it."

Collin pondered the comment for a moment. Being the son of district court judge Katrina Boudreaux Stallion, and then adopted by her husband, mega Attorney Matthew Stallion, he had big shoes to fill and an extraordinary family legacy to uphold. He didn't have the words to express that pursuing his own legal career came with some self-confidence issues he hadn't anticipated. "Mom's really excited about me working for Stallion Enterprises. But I'll be honest, Dad. I don't know if I'm ready for that."

"Your mom wants you to be happy, no matter what you choose to do. So, what is it you're thinking you want to do?"

"That's my problem. I'm not sure. I really don't have a clue." Collin's gaze was downcast as he drummed his fingers against the crystal glass resting on the table before him.

His father nodded. "May I make a suggestion?"

"Please. I can use all the advice I can get."

Matthew smiled. "There's a community organization called the Pro Bono Partnership of Dallas. They provide legal services to the underserved and the disadvantaged. Only a select few are added to their payroll, but they're always looking for good attorneys willing to donate their time to help. I think you should give it a try."

"It wouldn't be a salaried position, though?"

"Probably not, but it's a great way to spend your time until you figure out what you want to be doing. And you know how much we believe in being of service to others."

"What about my bills?"

"What bills?" Matthew eyed him with a raised brow.

"I know I don't have to pay rent or anything, and I'm blessed that I don't have any student loans to repay, but I don't want you and Mom covering my personal expenses. And I was hoping to get my own apartment at some point. I mean, the guesthouse is great and all, but what's it going to look like if I bring a girl home and Jake is hanging out the window, screaming my name? Or, worse, Mom is tracking who's coming and going!"

"Jake better not be hanging out any window!"

"You know what I mean."

"I do," Matthew said with a light chuckle. "Which is why you need to relax and trust me when I tell you it will all work out. Find out if the Pro Bono Partnership can use you. Then go from there."

Collin nodded, a slight degree of uncertainty lingering in his eyes. He did trust his father, but his future prospects still felt daunting. He took a sip of his own drink, wincing as the bitter fluid burned the back of his throat.

Matthew laughed, "You're not a scotch man, I take it!"

"Sorry, Pops! I'm more of a bourbon guy like Uncle Mark."

His father winked at him. "I'll be sure to pick up a bottle just for you. Now, tell me about these girls you're planning to bring home, hoping your mother won't be tracking!"

Pulling his new car past the gates of Stallion-Briscoe Ranch, Collin was surprised by the intensity of emotion that suddenly overwhelmed him. It happened every time he returned to his uncle's home. Stallion-Briscoe Ranch was well over eight hundred acres of working cattle ranch, an equestrian center and an entertainment complex that specialized in corporate and private client services. With the property being central to Austin, Houston, Dallas and Fort Worth, the ranch had made quite a name for itself.

Back in the day, Edward Briscoe, the ranch's original owner, had been one of the original black cowboys. Not long after the birth of his three daughters—Eden and the twins, Marla and Marah—he and his first wife had expanded their Texas longhorn operation, adding two twenty-thousand-square-foot event barns and a country bed-and-breakfast.

After Marah Briscoe's marriage to business tycoon John Stallion, Edward had gifted the property to his daughter and new son-in-law, her love for a Stallion ending the conflict that had brought the couple together in the first place. With her father wanting to sell the ranch, John Stallion wanting to buy the property and Marah interfering at every turn, their acquaintance had gotten off to a contentious start. Under the umbrella of Stallion Enterprises and managed by brothers Matthew, Mark, Luke and John, the ranch had grown exponentially. It was now a resource for several government programs that assisted children and families in need. It was a community center of sorts and a bright light in the Dallas area. But the ranch was still home to all the Stallions and the pride and joy of the family.

Eleven years ago, Collin had been sent to Stallion-Briscoe Ranch as a part of his court-ordered plea agreement for stealing Matthew Stallion's car. It was where he had found family and a sense of belonging. He'd grown up at the ranch, and returning to where it had all started for him punched him in the gut every time.

His father and his uncles were all standing on the front porch as he stepped out of his car. Pride registered over their expressions, broad chests pushed forward as they moved down the porch steps to greet him and inspect his ride.

"Congratulations, nephew!" Mark Stallion said as he wrapped Collin in a heavy bear hug.

John and Luke Stallion echoed the sentiment. "When did you get home, son?" his uncle John asked.

"Yesterday."

"Nice ride!" Luke exclaimed. "Somebody did something right."

"Collin actually went to college and studied," John said. He shot his brother a look. "And he completed his undergrad in three years. He didn't take the five-year route like some other people we know."

"Are you ever going to let that go?" Luke queried. "I've been out of school and managing my own division in the company for how many years now, and you still keep harping on the fact that it took me a little longer to find my way!"

Matthew chuckled, "When you pay him back for those extra semesters I'm sure he'll let it go."

"That would be a start," John said teasingly as they all laughed heartily.

Luke turned his attention back to his nephew. "So, what are your plans? You make any yet?"

"Still trying to figure it out," Collin answered as he shot his father a look.

Matthew nodded. "Collin might do some pro bono work while he gets himself acclimated. He doesn't know yet if corporate law is what he wants to do."

John nodded. "Nothing wrong with that. Take your time and don't rush into anything. Success comes when you love what you're doing, and it doesn't feel like work."

"Actually," Mark added, "I might be able to use you around here while you figure it out."

"Here?" Collin's eyes widened.

"We could use another mentor for our youth program. You went through it, so you'd be perfect. It's only part-time and it doesn't pay much, but it'll put some change into your pocket until you find something else."

Collin glanced at his father and Matthew shrugged, lifting his hands as if he were surrendering.

"I didn't say anything," Matthew said. "I told you everything will always work out when you need it to. You just need to have faith."

Mark looked from one to the other, a confused expression on his face. "What am I missing?"

Matthew laughed, patting his son on the back. Before either could respond, John's wife, Marah, called to them from the front porch. "Breakfast! Come eat, please!"

Collin slid back into the comfort of the family dynamics like he hadn't been away at school for three years earning a bachelor's degree in political science and another three earning a Juris Doctor. Summers when he hadn't taken classes, he had interned. First, for a private marketing and communications firm, then a local senator at the Capitol building, and for the past two summers, with Mass Legal Aid Services. The experiences had helped him grow and now he was home.

As the oldest grandchild in the family, he'd always heard his name called first and often. He was pleasantly surprised to see that his cousins and brother were now old enough to step up, the adults no longer looking to him first to run and fetch things or to corral the younger kids.

He sat between his father and his uncle Mark, listening as his aunt Marah's father told one of the bawdy jokes he was known for. The women were all shaking their heads and admonishing the old man to keep things G-rated for the many little ears hanging on to every word he was saying, while the youngsters hoped he would slip up and say something out of turn.

Looking around the table, Collin was in awe of how everyone had seemed to age, still themselves, but not. Grandpa Edward sat at the head of the table. He'd been gray before, but his head of silver hair had thinned considerably. Shortly after the death of Juanita, his second wife, he'd suffered a stroke. Collin had been in high school then, and although it had been a few years since the old man's health had failed him, Grandpa Edward still struggled with his speech. He also walked with a limp, and one arm was locked tight to his side, permanently disabled. He was particularly cantankerous, too.

Marah fussed over him despite his constant bellowing to be left to his own devices. He loved to spend most of his time in the playroom on the second floor, watching the younger children play, and slipping five-dollar bills into their pockets when their parents weren't looking. He and Collin had often fished together in the pond on the other side of the large estate and Collin hoped to be able to do that with the old man again.

John and Marah sat on either side of the patriarch, Marah fretting and John beaming with pride as he sat back, observing them all. Once or twice he and Collin exchanged a look and Collin knew he embodied every hope and dream his uncle had ever had for all the members of his family. John's daughter, Gabrielle, and Mark's daughter, Irene, sat between their fathers, the two teens still bickering about nothing. Despite their age difference—Irene being older by four years—they were the best of friends, and when they weren't fighting, the two girls were huddled together, whispering and laughing about something.

Irene's mother, his aunt Michelle, affectionately known as Mitch to family and friends, and his aunt Joanne, Luke's wife, were refilling empty platters as they puttered between the kitchen and the oversize dining table. Collin's mother and his aunt Phaedra, the only sister to Matthew, Mark, Luke and John, and married to his mother's oldest brother, Mason Boudreaux, were in the other room rounding up the kids around their own table.

Aunt Phaedra and Uncle Mason had three children: Cole, Addison and Fletcher Boudreaux. Jake was giving them orders, lording over the younger kids simply because he was older. Collin couldn't help but think he'd taught him well. He turned his attention back to Grandpa Edward.

The old man could barely hold his exuberance as he shared his joke. "It was spring in the Old West. The cowboys rode the trails looking for cattle that had survived the winter. As one cowboy's horse went around the narrow trail, it came upon a rattlesnake warming itself in the spring sunshine. The horse reared, and the cowboy drew his six-gun to shoot the snake. 'Hold on there, partner,' said the snake. 'Don't shoot! I'm an enchanted rattlesnake, and if you don't shoot me, I'll give you any three wishes you want.'

"The cowboy decided to take a chance. He knew

he was safely out of the snake's striking range. He said, 'Okay, first, I'd like to have a face like Denzel, then I'd like a body like that wrestler they call the Rock, and finally, I'd like sexual equipment like this here horse I'm riding.' The rattlesnake said, 'All right, when you get back to the bunkhouse you'll have all three wishes.' The cowboy turned his horse around and galloped at full speed all the way to the bunkhouse. He dismounted and went straight inside to the mirror.

"Staring back at him in the mirror was the face of Denzel. He ripped the shirt off his back and revealed bulging, rippling muscles, just like the Rock. Really excited now, he tore down his jeans, looked at his crotch and shouted, 'Oh, my God, I was riding the mare!'"

Collin burst out laughing with the older members of the family. Irene and Gabby exchanged a look.

"I don't get it," fifteen-year-old Gabby said, looking around the table. Her eyes were wide, and bewilderment swept over her face.

"You don't need to get it," John answered. He raised his eyebrows and tossed his wife a look.

Marah only shook her head in response.

Irene leaned to whisper in Gabrielle's ear. Both girls suddenly burst out laughing.

Collin was suddenly reminded of his high school graduation, when the girls had been eight and twelve and had thought it amusing to announce at family breakfast that they'd seen him playing with his penis after bursting into his room unannounced. He'd been mortified with embarrassment. Despite his insistence that he'd only been adjusting himself in his boxer briefs as he dressed, the moment had become fodder for too many jokes among the family. He stole a glance at Luke, who was grinning at him.

He shook his head. "Don't go there, Uncle Luke."

"You must have read my mind."

Matthew laughed, "I'm sure we all thought the same thing, but I agree with Collin. Time to let that go."

"Time to change the subject," Marah intoned. "Everyone needs to eat up. We need to get ready to leave for church and from the looks of things some of you need a little more God than others!" She narrowed her gaze on the girls, her head waving from side to side.

Gabrielle rolled her eyes, then zeroed in on Collin. Everyone had been extolling praises on him, admonishing the younger crowd to be more like their big cousin. She wasn't quite as impressed and had no qualms about saying so. Picking on Collin had been her and Irene's favorite thing to do for as long as she could remember.

"Collin, can we ride to church with you? We want to ride in your new car."

He gave her a look back, not easily swayed by her sweet smile and the doe-eyed gaze she was giving him. He had no doubt that Trouble One and Trouble Two had other plans up their sleeves that probably involved him driving them to the mall after Sunday service. Before he could respond, his uncle Mason bellowed from the other end of the table, saving him from what surely would have turned into a moment of discord, with him being the villain.

"Sorry, girls, but Collin is chauffeuring us boys to church this morning. He promised me, Jake, Fletcher and Cole a ride. You two will have to catch him next time."

Collin shot his uncle a grateful look. He winked at his cousins, and the girls pouted profusely at having their plans usurped. "Sorry, girls," he said as he reached for the platter of bacon and took a second helping.

"What about after church?" Irene asked, shifting forward as she batted her lashes at him.

"I'm going horseback riding. I haven't been down to the stables since I got home. I need to check on my horse and I'm sure the stalls probably need mucking and the horses need to be brushed. Maybe you two could come and help me out?"

"Yuck!" both said in unison, their faces twisted with aversion.

"Let's not," Irene said with a shake of her head.

"And just say we did!" Gabrielle concluded as she finished her favorite cousin's new favorite saying.

Breakfast was the best of everything Collin loved about his family. Laughter was abundant, advice was as generous as the food, and standing there in the shadows of the men he loved most, Collin knew that whatever worries he might have had, he had more than his fair share of support to help him get through. Home had never felt better.

Chapter 2

London Jacobs eyed her two best friends with a raised brow. The two women stood in her office, peeking through the closed blinds and out toward the conference room. They were giggling like grade-schoolers. Paula Graves and Felicia Tyson waved her inside, closing the door as she stepped over the threshold.

"What's going on?" London asked as she moved to the executive's chair made of leather, dropping her purse into the desk drawer and her leather attaché on the desktop.

Paula waved a hand in her direction. "Good morning! The new guy is here."

"And he's absolutely gorgeous!" Felicia exclaimed. "There's no way I'm going to be able to work with him and stay focused."

London laughed, "You two are unbelievable!" She

moved to the glass and pulled the blinds open. Just as she did, she came face-to-face with the firm's director of operations, who was standing on the other side of the glass. Perry Swann was headed toward the conference room. He came to an abrupt halt, his eyes shifting to stare at the three of them. He suddenly gestured for their attention, waving them to follow him.

"This can't be good," Felicia said. She shot London a look.

"It's not even nine o'clock yet," Paula muttered, her head waving.

London gave the man a nod and slight smile, then watched as he turned and disappeared into the meeting room. She focused back on her friends, her eyes rolling skyward. "I'm sure it's fine. You two need to stop being so dramatic."

"After the weekend I've had, I deserve to be dramatic," Felicia said. "Gary came home and all he did was argue with the old people," she said, referring to her brother. Her wayward sibling had been a boil on the family's good name since his first arrest when he was sixteen. Their father was a state representative who'd focused his election on the social evils of addiction and crime. Representative Tyson had lifted his only son up as an example of his understanding of the plight facing the families in his district. London could only begin to imagine their turmoil with Gary's current release for yet another petty crime. She nodded, reaching to give the young woman a hug.

The three women exhaled simultaneously, low gusts of air blowing past glossy lips. Their gazes shifted back and forth, and then they laughed.

London moved to the door and pulled it open. "Let's go meet the new guy," she said.

* * *

"Ladies, good morning," Perry said as he greeted the trio with a stern stare. He met each of their gazes as he beckoned them into the room.

"Good morning, Perry," London said, narrowing her gaze as she met his. "To what do we owe the honor this morning?"

Most of the staff was sitting around, sipping cups of coffee and eating doughnuts from Jarams Artisan Donuts. The shop was a north Dallas fixture that specialized in pretty confections. Three white baker's boxes held fried rings of dough filled with an assortment of creams, drizzled with glazes and sprinkled with powdered sugar, nuts and candies. They scented the whole room with an abundance of sweet fragrance.

Perry gestured toward the other end of the space and the man standing there, shaking hands. "I figured since we were having a staff meeting and welcoming our new attorney, it wouldn't hurt to kick off the week with a treat."

London gave him a slight nod. Perry had only recently assumed responsibility for the law firm and was still finding his balance with the staff. He had a reputation for being uptight and a tad anal. He was a stickler for punctuality and usually frowned on them not using every minute of their time working. She couldn't help wondering what was so special about the new guy that warranted the party-like welcome.

Perry seemed to read her mind. His voice dropped an octave as he leaned in to whisper, "His name is Collin Stallion. Heir to Stallion Enterprises and the infamous Stallion family fortune. His mother is also…"

"Judge Katrina Stallion. She serves the 232nd District Criminal Court. I'm familiar with her. She has a large presence at the Dallas Girls Club. She's been mentoring there for years." There was a hint of awe in London's tone.

Perry nodded his head excitedly. "Yes! And the Stallion family have been great supporters of all our efforts. His father has volunteered his services here many times and John Stallion sits on the board."

London barely gave the man a hint of a smile in response. There weren't many in Dallas who didn't know the Stallion name or reputation. Stallion Enterprises had been started by John Stallion, one of four brothers. It was a successful corporate empire built on commercial real estate and development, as well as a shipping company, numerous entertainment interests and a lengthy chain of hotels. The brothers—Matthew, Mark, Luke and John—had grown the endeavor into a multi-billion-dollar enterprise.

"Let me introduce you," Perry started, just as his secretary called his name, gesturing frantically for his attention.

"Please, go," London said. "I'll introduce myself."

As Perry hurried out of the room, London turned to eye the man who had most of the women, and a few of the men, fawning for his attention. Paula and Felicia had already shaken hands with him and both now sat at the table, doughnuts in hand as they whispered like two hens. She shook her head at them as Paula gestured in his direction, winking teasingly.

Collin Stallion was definitely as good-looking as both her friends had claimed. He was tall, easily standing over six feet. He was dressed in a silk suit that fitted him to perfection, the dark navy flattering his warm beige complexion. A white dress shirt, red paisley necktie and black patent-leather dress shoes completed the ensemble. The shoes were expensive and highly polished, and told London everything she needed to know about the man. His hair was dreadlocked, the light, sandy-brown strands falling just past his shoulders. He'd captured the length in a neat ponytail that hung down the center of his back.

Collin was suddenly staring directly at her. His eyes were a deep shade of amber with gold flecks that shimmered behind lengthy lashes. London heard herself gasp, a swift inhale of air that sounded as if she'd been punched square in the stomach. He was dazzling, emanating a glow of kindness that felt infectious. It had captivated everyone in the room and even London was finding it difficult to resist.

She snatched her gaze from his and took two deep breaths before shifting her eyes back to his. He was still staring, a bright smile filling his chiseled face. He was exquisite, and despite her every effort, he took her breath away. Needing a distraction, she turned her attention back to his shoes, which, she recognized, were designed by the contemporary shoemaker Maison Corthay. The crisply polished leather easily cost what she paid in rent for three months. She hated that she knew that. Her obsession with designer fashion was a guilty pleasure few were aware of. Nor did they know that most of her own designer-label possessions were previous years' releases found at local thrift and consignment shops.

Everyone was familiar with the Stallion family's reputation. Collin's parents were at the top of their game in the legal profession. His uncles had built one of the largest black-owned corporations in the world, each of them making one of *Forbes* magazine's rich lists annually. The family's wealth was impressive and mind-boggling. Collin Stallion's silver spoon came with gold medallions and diamond-encrusted embellishments. So, what was he really doing there? Her name being spoken pulled at her attention. She looked up with a start, then forced a smile to her face as she lifted her eyes to find Perry and Collin standing right in front of her. Her gaze met Collin's and locked.

"London is one of our staff attorneys. She litigates postconviction cases here in the Dallas area. She's been a top litigator for us for almost two years now," Perry said.

He went on to complete the introduction. "London, this is Collin Stallion. Attorney Stallion was in Boston prior to passing the bar here in Texas. He's bypassing an opportunity to practice corporate law to help us here with our innocence initiative. You two will be working closely together."

"It's a pleasure to meet you, Mr. Stallion. Welcome aboard."

"Please, call me Collin," he said as his palm slid gently against hers.

London was surprised to discover his hands weren't as soft and pasty as she had expected. His skin was slightly calloused, his fingers were strong, and his palm was surprisingly hot. A wave of heat surged in her like a firestorm. London was taken aback by the magnitude of it and practically snatched her hand from his.

The furl of his lips deepened, showcasing the prettiest set of snow-white teeth. "Thank you," he said, his deep voice thick and rich like blackstrap molasses. "I look forward to our working together."

London tossed him a nod of her head. "I think I'll grab a doughnut," she said as she stepped back, Perry already pulling another attorney forward to make an introduction.

A doughnut? Did I really just say that? London shook her head as she eased over to the other side of the room. *I should have kept looking at his damn shoes*, she thought.

Both Paula and Felicia were grinning foolishly at her as she sat down.

"That looked like it went well," Felicia said, her laughter teasing. "You didn't trip on anything."

"That glazed deer-in-headlights look you have isn't pretty, though," Paula said. "There's a hint of desperation, just a tiny hint," she added teasingly, gesturing with her thumb and forefinger.

"Neither of you is funny," London said, a frown pulling the lines of her face downward. Her eyes rolled as she poked at a chocolate-iced doughnut Felicia pushed toward her.

"Actually, I think it went very well. He's still staring at you," Paula quipped.

"Staring at who?" London asked, her eyes widening.

Paula laughed, "At you." She gestured with her head, throwing the slightest of nods in the man's direction.

London tossed a quick glance over her shoulder. Collin *was* still staring and when he saw her looking, he smiled.

* * *

Collin gazed from his office toward Attorney Jacobs's, hoping against all odds to catch a glimpse of the beautiful woman. London Jacobs had taken his breath away and it had truly been a struggle to contain his interest. She'd captured his attention the moment she'd entered the conference room. Despite her obvious efforts to mask her supermodel looks, she was stunning. She wore the barest hint of makeup, her face adorned with just a little eyeliner and rose-tinted lip gloss. She wore a charcoal-gray silk suit, the blazer closed with four buttons and belted around her waist. Her hair was pulled back into a slick ponytail. She was a wisp of a woman, petite in stature, with hints of curves in all the right places. She was the sweetest confection, with a mouth that begged to be kissed. Despite his best efforts at self-control, he couldn't stop thinking about kissing London Jacobs's delicate mouth or the dreamy look in her eyes when she'd looked at him.

There was a purity in her expression, and something very refreshing in her appraisal of him. She hadn't seemed at all impressed, neither the reputation of his family name nor his looks swaying her attention. Usually women fell all over him, influenced by one, the other or both. Women his father and uncles had often told him to be wary of.

While there had been a few who had been excessively attentive to him, London had appeared genuinely disinterested until those moments they'd locked gazes and held on. And when they'd connected, it wasn't what he saw but more about a feeling that singed the edges of his spirit as heat coursed up his spine. There'd been fire in the dark orbs of her eyes and it had ignited something deep in his core that was still simmering on a slow burn.

Perry suddenly stood in the doorway, gesturing for his attention, an index finger waving as if it was unhinged. "Collin, if I can grab you for minute, please." He shook a manila file folder in the other hand.

"Certainly," Collin said, rising from his seat.

He followed as Perry led the way to London's office. Perry knocked before he pushed his way inside.

Collin paused at the entrance, and when she gestured with a polite smile he felt a quiver of something he couldn't quite name billow through his midsection.

London greeted them both warmly. "Gentlemen, please, have a seat. How can I help you?"

Perry looked from her to him with a raised brow. "They've set a trial date for the Jerome James case. It's been decided that Collin will sit second chair with you."

Although his internships had given him a wealth of experience, Collin couldn't help feeling like he might be out of his element. The boxes of case files that littered his office seemed to be growing exponentially as he shifted through the multitude of folders that detailed everything about Mr. Jerome James, a former community activist incarcerated for the murder of his wife. James had always maintained his innocence and had become somewhat of a legend in the community. Affording him a new trial had taken the innocence coalition eight years of one court motion after another to secure. Countless hours and the efforts of a large task force had laid the foundation for what would soon come. Collin blew a soft sigh, moving yet another folder of documents to his completed pile as he pulled one from the to-be-read pile. Leaning back in his seat, he made himself comfortable.

He'd been reading for a good hour when he looked up to find Attorney Jacobs staring at him. She stood in his doorway with her arms crossed tightly over her chest, a curious furrow on her brow. Amusement pierced his spirit as he stared back. She hadn't had much to say to him since he'd been assigned to work with her. For the last few weeks, the little conversation between them had been limited to polite chatter and her admonishments for him to update himself on the details of the case as she dropped yet another box of files onto his desk. That she was standing there, looking like she was interested in a real conversation, was clearly progress.

"Good morning," he said, his eyes lifting with his bright smile.

"Good morning. Weren't you in that same position when we all left you here last night?"

He chuckled, "I probably was. I need to make sure I'm up to speed, so I left late and came in early."

"Interesting," she said, the word coming on a low gust of air past red-tinted lips.

"Why is that interesting?"

She ignored his question as she glanced down to her wristwatch. "Mr. James was transferred to county jail yesterday. He'll be held there until his trial is over. I'm headed over to talk to him about his court date. Would you like to join me?"

Collin's smile widened. "I'd like that. I'd like that very much!"

An hour later, the two were on their way to the Lew Sterrett Justice Center of Dallas. Despite his offer to drive, London has insisted on taking her own car, so he settled back against the leather seats of her SUV and tried to enjoy the ride. He'd tried to pull the woman into conversation, but London wasn't interested in talking. He'd listened as she'd taken phone calls, the Bluetooth connection echoing through the car interior. Then she'd hummed along with the radio, completely lost in her own thoughts. By the time they pulled into the parking lot of the correctional facility she'd done everything imaginable to keep from conversing with him.

"Are you always so rude?" he asked.

London shut down the car engine as she turned toward him, the question surprising her. Because she had been rude. She just hadn't expected to be called out on it and there was no way she could explain to the man that he had her feeling like a high schooler with her first crush. She took a deep breath. "Excuse me?"

"Rude. Are you always so rude?"

"I didn't realize..."

"You have gone out of your way not to speak with me despite my efforts to talk to you and maybe discuss the case. You've talked to your secretary, some friend named Joan and your mother. But you've barely said three words to me since we left the office."

London's eyes danced across his face. Something she didn't recognize surged through the pit of her stomach, like an electric current stuck on high. "I apologize. It was never my intent to be rude to you."

"Except you were."

She took another deep breath, filling her lungs with air and then blowing it out slowly. Her gaze was still flitting back and forth over the intense stare he was giving her. "Why are you here?" she suddenly asked,

an air of attitude in her tone. "What are you trying
to prove?"

His brow shifted upward. "I'm not trying to prove
anything. I'm just trying to do the best job I can."

"But why here? There are hundreds of attorneys who apply and are denied, and you slide in on
your family name and no doubt a big donation from
Mommy and Daddy. You barely have any litigation
experience under your belt!" She threw her hands up
in frustration.

Collin bristled, the comment hitting a nerve he
hadn't known he possessed. There was no denying
that the Stallion name opened doors that might have
otherwise been closed. Although he had never purposely used his family connections to garner favor,
admittedly it did happen sometimes. But when chal-
lenged, he was more than capable of holding his own
against the naysayers. He shifted his gaze from hers,
finally breaking the connection that he'd been holding with no effort.

A moment passed between them before he answered.
"So maybe I do have something to prove. Maybe it's
about what I'm able to accomplish, in spite of my name.
I like to think I'm a good attorney, even with my limited
experience, and I'm here because I believe in what the
firm stands for. I want to help, and I had hoped to be
able to do that without people judging me before they
took the time to know me."

London suddenly felt foolish. Her eyes flitted back
and forth, and she struggled to find the words to apologize and not dig herself into an even bigger hole. "I'm
sorry," she said finally, her tone dropping low. "You're
right. I should not have judged you. If it's okay with

you, I'd like to start over." She extended her hand to shake his. "It's a pleasure to meet you, Attorney Stallion. I look forward to our working together."

Collin smiled sweetly as he gripped her fingers against his palm. He gave her a slight nod of his head. "Thank you, Counselor. I appreciate that. I know I can learn a lot from you and I'm grateful for the opportunity."

With his court case pending, their client had been transferred from the state's maximum-security prison in Ferguson, Texas, to the county jailhouse in Dallas. Back in his day, Jerome James had been a popular community activist, known for frequently going toe-to-toe with local law enforcement. His frequent protests and rallies against the legal vanguard he alleged was corrupt and immoral had made him more enemies than friends.

When he hadn't been fighting for the rights of those most marginalized and disenfranchised, he'd been a respected automotive repair technician working at a local garage. He had also been a loving husband and father, living a blessed life, with the house, dog and picket fence. Things had turned for him when his wife, a beloved schoolteacher, was found murdered in their bed. He'd been convicted of that murder, despite more evidence pointing to his innocence than his guilt. It had been a miscarriage of justice of monumental proportions.

Collin had studied the detailed police reports. The couple had just celebrated their twelfth wedding anniversary. They were also anxiously awaiting the birth of their third child. James had left for work early that day, kissing his wife goodbye as she'd slept. Later that morning, Mary James's body was found in their bedroom. She'd been sexually assaulted and bludgeoned to death. Despite no tangible evidence, the prosecution had argued he'd raped and murdered his wife after an argument. Months later, James had been convicted of the crime, sentenced to life in prison with no possibility of parole. Years of appeals and a mountain of discovery had since turned up potentially exculpatory evidence pointing to Mr. James's innocence that the prosecution had concealed. Now Jerome James was getting a second chance at justice.

Collin hadn't known what to expect as they checked in and proceeded through the prison's inner maze to the visiting room where they waited for their client. London had briefed him on the case's procedural tactics that she had been personally involved in overseeing, and there was an air of pride in her voice as she detailed the decisions she'd been proudest of making.

"Our original motion for DNA testing on items of evidence from the crime scene omitted a bloody towel that had been found in the woods behind the family home. Unfortunately, those tests could not exclude Mr. Jerome as the source of the DNA collected from the bed."

"Why was the towel not included?"

"A previous attorney on the case missed adding it to the evidence list when the motion was filed."

"And that was three years ago, correct?"

"Yes, the motion that was filed most recently includes that towel and I'm willing to bet the tests will prove conclusively that he didn't harm his wife. That someone else was present in the family bed."

Before Collin could respond, the heavy iron door swung open and Jerome James was ushered inside. He was a big bear of a man, years of prison yard work and cell-block weight training having sculpted his body into hard lean muscle. With his salt-and-pepper hair and full beard, he looked very distinguished, and entered with an air of confidence that actually surprised Collin. He gave the younger man a nod, eyeing him with interest.

The guard gestured for him to take a seat, and after securing his handcuffs to the chain bolted in the center of the table, he exited the room and closed the door behind him. Mr. James shifted his gaze toward London.

"It's a pleasure to see you again, Ms. Jacobs. To what do I owe the honor? I was actually surprised when they moved me."

London sat down, placing her hands atop his. "You've been granted a new trial, Mr. James. The state of Texas has set aside your original verdict and we're going to be able to present your case with the evidence that wasn't included in the first trial."

Mr. James said nothing, seeming to ponder the information for a good few minutes. Then he nodded his head and turned his attention on Collin. "And who might you be, young man?"

Collin dropped into the seat beside London. "Collin Stallion, sir. It's a pleasure to meet you."

"Collin will be sitting second chair on your case," London interjected. "He just recently joined the Pro Bono Partnership."

"Where'd you go to school?" Mr. James questioned.

"I graduated from Harvard, sir."

"Why didn't you go to a historically black college or university? Our HBCUs don't get nearly enough recognition or love."

"Legacy, sir. Both my parents were Harvard alum."

The old man eyed him intently. "Stallion? Who's your father, son?"

"Matthew Stallion, sir."

There was a moment as Mr. James appeared to be searching his thoughts. After a minute or two of reflection he simply nodded his head. He turned his attention back to London. "Would you please get a message to my son? Tell him I'm here, please. Hopefully, he'll be able to come see me now that I'm closer."

"We can call your daughter, too, if you'd like," London said.

The man shook his head. "My Jackie lives in New York now. She has a good job with some fashion company there. I don't want y'all upsetting her. I'm sure her brother will tell her whatever needs to be told."

"Yes, sir," London said. "Do you have any questions for us, Mr. James?"

He shook his head, his expression blank.

London nodded. Rising from her seat, she knocked on the door, and the guard responded almost immediately. "We will probably be back sometime early next week," she said. "If you need anything before then, just call."

Mr. James nodded. "Just get that message to my son. I don't need anything else."

The guard gestured for them to leave. Mr. James called after Collin.

"Yes, sir?"

"Please, tell your father hello for me."

* * *

"He wasn't excited," Collin said, the words spoken aloud before he could catch them.

London cut an eye in his direction.

He eyed her back, his shoulders shrugging slightly. "I thought he would have been more excited."

She blew a soft sigh. "The first time I met him I thought the same thing. But when you think about it, for the last thirty-two years he's known nothing but disappointment. His wife dies. He's barely able to grieve before he's being accused of her murder. The trial was a travesty. He's convicted and incarcerated. He loses his children. Every countermotion his defense team made either failed or was rejected. And now we're going to make him relive it all again, with no assurances of a different outcome. Unfortunately, he's a black man in a judicial system that doesn't value his life. When you consider the odds are stacked against him, and us, he can't afford to be excited. If we lose, he could very well be given the lethal injection this time."

Collin nodded. "Sounds like you and I have our work cut out."

"You and I will not lose this case and I don't care what it takes," she said emphatically.

He met the look she tossed him, her eyes slightly misted. "I'm going to hold you to that," he said.

"I haven't eaten anything today," she said. "If you don't have plans, why don't we grab some lunch? I know you've been through most of the files already and I can answer your questions and fill in any blanks for you."

"I'd like that," Collin said. "I would like that a lot."

She smiled. "Don't get too excited, Stallion. I plan to grill you, too. I need to see what you do and don't know."

His father was in his office poring over a mountain of paperwork when Collin entered the family home. It was late, and his mother and brother were already in bed. Matthew looked up from what he was doing and gave his son a quick nod of his head.

"Hey there! You're keeping some late hours!"

"Working on a case. There's a lot to catch up on."

Matthew leaned back in his chair, folding his hands together in his lap. "So, how are things going with your new job?"

"I like it. I really like it a lot. Met my client today. Apparently, he knows you. He asked me to tell you hello."

"Really? Who is he?"

"Jerome James. He's been incarcerated for the murder of his wife. He's been granted a new trial and I'm going to be sitting second chair."

Matthew's eyes dropped as he fell into thought. When he looked back up Collin was eyeing him curiously. He gave his son a slight smile. "Jerome and his wife, Mary, went to school with us. Jerome graduated with your uncle John and Mary graduated with me. Back in the day we were big supporters of the causes Jerome took up. Even marched the streets with him a time or two. He was a good man. Everything about that case was tragic."

"The case file reads like a witch hunt."

"The racial climate back then was rough, and Jerome loved to make waves. He was not popular with the local police or the politicians. He wanted change and he fought hard to make that happen. Remind me, who was the original prosecutor?"

"Victor Wells."

"Newly appointed *Texas Supreme Court Justice* Victor Wells?"

Collin nodded. "The one and only. Do you know him?"

Matthew nodded. A look of foreboding washed over his expression. The same look that Collin had seen on London's face when they had first discussed the case and Wells's name had been mentioned. It had given Collin pause and when he'd asked about it she'd dismissed him, insisting that there wasn't anything amiss that he needed to be concerned with. "Yes, I do," Matthew finally answered.

"Is there something about Justice Wells that I should know?" Collin questioned.

Matthew hesitated for a quick second as if there was more that he wanted to say, but he didn't elaborate. He just shook his head no.

"Any advice?"

"Just be smart and make sure you do your due diligence. And no matter what happens, do not be intimidated."

Collin nodded as his father continued.

"Who's your first chair?" Matthew asked.

"Attorney London Jacobs. She's been with the initiative for a few years and litigating their big cases for the last two years." Collin's eyes were bright, his entire face lifting with the smile that spread from ear to ear. He thought back to his day and the shift in her attitude toward him between breakfast and lunch. She'd been exceptionally open and forthcoming as they'd discussed the case. She'd asked his opinion and had seemed genuinely interested in his answers. An encounter that had started out tensely had transitioned nicely to a pleasant exchange.

Matthew smiled back. "I know Ms. Jacobs. She's quite impressive. Jerome will be well served."

"I think we're going to be a great team," Collin said, a hint of excitement in his tone.

His father nodded, his head bobbing up and down slowly. He stared at his oldest child but said nothing, bemusement painting his expression.

"What?" Collin asked, suddenly feeling self-conscious.

Matthew shook his head. "Nothing, son. Nothing at all."

Chapter 3

London was pleasantly surprised by Collin's work ethic. He asked questions she hadn't expected, even giving her reason to pause as she pondered a few of his suggestions. He was formidable, and it was apparent he was as dedicated to Mr. James's interests as she was.

She hadn't expected to like him as much as she did. She found herself looking forward to seeing him when she arrived at the office. Since that first lunch, they'd eaten lunch together a few times, that hour of personal time quickly becoming the highlight of her day.

When he burst through the door of her office, his excitement was palpable. "We got the DNA tests back!" he exclaimed, waving the file over his head. He passed her the manila folder, reciting the results as she flipped through the documents. "According to the lab, the DNA on the towel belonged to Mary James and an unknown male. It was also a perfect match to the DNA from the sperm left on the bedsheets. They're running it through the CODIS database now to see if we can get a hit and hopefully a name. Keep your fingers crossed, but I think we just got the big break in the case we needed."

London pumped a fist, her own excitement spreading across her face. She squealed with glee, resisting the urge to throw herself into his arms and jump for joy. "Yes, yes, yes!" she exclaimed. "Make sure you add this to our evidence list. We'll need to send copies over to the prosecutor's office, as well. Full disclosure. I don't want them making any claims about our impeding their due process."

"I already took care of it," he answered. "I also filed a Public Information Act request. I want to get a look at what other documents were in the prosecution's file that might have been withheld at the time of his trial."

"You think there's something there that can help us?"

"I don't know. It's just a gut feeling I have."

London nodded. "I trust your instincts, Counselor."

Collin crossed his arms over his broad chest. "A compliment. I'm touched!"

London laughed, "An attorney with jokes!"

"One or two," he teased.

She shook her head. "You available for lunch later?"

"I actually need to go down to the courthouse and

then the law library. Are you by chance available for dinner?"

Her eyebrows lifted, a hint of surprise tinting her cheeks. "D-dinner? I'm not... Well... I don't..." she stammered.

"It's just dinner, London. We've had lunch together every day for the past few weeks. Dinner would be no different."

She rolled her eyes skyward. "The question surprised me is all. I don't usually..."

He stalled her comment. "What? You don't usually eat dinner? Do you have something against the evening meal?" His expression was smug as he eyed her intently, the invitation still hanging heavily between them.

"I would love to have dinner with you," she said finally.

Collin grinned. "I can pick you up at seven."

"Why don't I meet you?" she answered. "I think that would be more appropriate."

Collin laughed, "Whatever you say, Counselor."

"What about Jimmy's Food Store?"

"We're doing dinner, not lunch, Ms. Jacobs. Let's say Truluck's on McKinney Avenue at seven. I'll call and reserve us a table."

London thought to argue but Collin was out the door before she could respond. She took a step after him, suddenly thinking that dinner might be a mistake, but before she could follow after him and cancel, Perry was summoning her to a meeting. As she headed in that direction, two thoughts crossed her mind. *This dinner is a huge mistake.* And *what the hell am I going to wear?*

* * *

Paula and Felicia were pulling clothes out of London's closet like they were shopping at Premium Outlets's bargain basement sale. Dresses were flying from one side of the bedroom to the other, all landing in the center of her queen-size bed, if not on the floor.

"You can never go wrong with a little black dress," Paula said.

Felicia jumped up and down excitedly. "How about that lace number you bought for that thing last year with what's his name that you backed out of at the last minute? You know which dress I'm talking about," she said, looking from London to Paula.

Paula laughed. "I am deeply disturbed that I do know exactly what dress you're talking about," she said as she rushed back to the closet, searching frantically through London's wardrobe. "The black lace, slightly off the shoulder, that stopped at her knees. That dress was hot!"

"I am not wearing black lace!" London exclaimed, eyeing them both like they'd lost their minds. "This is not a date."

"Like hell it isn't!" Felicia exclaimed. "Dinner at Truluck's Seafood Steak and Crab House is definitely a date."

"Dinner with a man that fine is definitely a date!" Paula added.

London reached for her cell phone. "That's it. I'm canceling," she said as she began to scroll through her contact list.

Felicia snatched the device from her hands. "You're doing no such thing."

"Why in the world would you cancel?" Paula asked,

finally laying her hands on that black lace. She held the dress up for the other two to see. "Now, this is special!"

London shook her head. "Oh, hell no! I am not wearing that dress and I don't care how cute it is. That is not the impression I'm trying to make. I'm wearing a suit."

Felicia shrugged. "You might be right. That dress says you want to get laid. But then again—" she pretended to slap her forehead before continuing "—you *do* want to get laid!" she laughed heartily.

London was not amused, and she said so. "You're not helping!"

Paula held up a second dress. "This is what you're wearing," she said. "This is perfect!"

The other two women turned to stare. Paula held up a form-fitting sheath dress in a simple floral print with the neckline, sleeves and hem piped in black. It was simple, elegant and a favorite of London's that she had yet to wear, the price tag still hanging from the dress label at the zipper.

"Very pretty!" Felicia exclaimed.

London nodded. "That's not bad. That might work."

"You need to get dressed," Paula admonished. "It's already six o'clock and you're going to hit traffic with your luck."

Thirty minutes later London stood in front of her full-length mirror, admiring her reflection. Felicia had twisted her natural hair into an updo that flattered her slight frame and Paula had perfected her makeup, adding just enough color to her face to brighten her eyes and give her a less casual appearance. Her two besties stood huddled together like proud parents sending her off to the prom. They were teary eyed and emotional, and they made her laugh.

"You're going to blow him away," Felicia said.

"You look fabulous!" Paula added.

"You two really need to get yourselves a life," London said, her cheeks a brilliant shade of bright red.

Paula laughed with her. "We're living vicariously through you."

"Which is why you need to get you some tonight," Felicia added. "I put condoms in your purse, just in case."

London shook her head. "Lock the door when you leave, please," she said, throwing them both a look. "I'll call you both when I get home."

Her friends grinned. "Just have a good time," they both echoed simultaneously.

The drive to the restaurant was fraught with energy London hadn't expected to feel. Despite her efforts to show indifference about meeting up with Collin, she was actually very excited. And anxious. Nervous tension cramped her stomach and had her perspiring like she'd just run a marathon. For the life of her she couldn't begin to explain it if she tried.

London was no stranger to dating. She did it regularly, with a fair degree of success. She enjoyed the repartee, the subtle teasing and flirtation, and on occasion, mind-blowing sex without commitment. After the experience of one serious relationship having gone very badly, she had no interest whatsoever in a long-term relationship and quickly dismissed any man who wasn't willing to play by the rules she established. And London had a long list of rules.

The men she dated had to be adequately employed, motivated to be successful, politically savvy, philanthropically invested in others, considerate of her grassroots mind-set, respectful of their elders and women, and not overtly religious since it had been some time since she'd last seen the inside of anyone's church. There was no kissing on the first date. There had to be a minimum of five dates before she even contemplated being intimate with a man. She didn't do last-minute invitations and expected outings to be planned well in advance. She was not a fan of spontaneity and she hated surprises. She never invited a man to her home, never had sex with him in her bed and never spent the night in his bed unless it was a planned getaway in a luxury hotel.

She could be fastidious, obsessive, slightly anal and not always as accommodating as she expected her male counterparts to be. She was a handful for most men and unapologetic about it. Maintaining control ensured her heart didn't get broken, she didn't get hurt and the relationships that didn't work could end as amicably as she needed them to.

Now she was headed to dinner with a man who had no idea about her rule book, and she hadn't had an opportunity to ensure he was willing to play by her rules. But it wasn't a date, she thought, fighting the urge to turn her car around and go back home. It was dinner and one meal couldn't possibly hurt either of them.

Collin stood outside of Truluck's, pacing anxiously back and forth as he waited for London to arrive. He hadn't returned to the office after leaving the law library and he hadn't called her, not wanting to give her the opportunity to change her mind. He had learned enough about London Jacobs to theorize she would have called by now if she intended to cancel. He could only begin to imagine how she was rationalizing their sharing a meal. Apparently, she was particular about who she dated, and he imagined that despite the friendship blooming between them, he hadn't yet made it to her short list. But he had high hopes.

From the first moment he'd laid eyes on her he'd been smitten. Everything about London warmed his spirit and when he was in her presence he'd found himself feeling like a puppy desperate for attention. He would have been happy with a slight scratch behind his ears and if he were lucky, a gentle tummy rub. But London wasn't partial to giving anything or anyone attention that didn't have something to do with a legal brief. He couldn't help wondering if she even liked dogs and he didn't imagine her to be particularly fond of cats. He laughed at the absurdity of his own analogy.

Despite his optimism he sensed that she might not be so interested in him. If there was someone else in her life whom she was dating, she kept it a closely guarded secret. Not even her two best friends in the office could be coaxed to spill that bit of tea. If he had competition, he didn't know it. He had no clue whom he might be up against if he had to battle for her time and attention. But he wasn't deterred by the unknown.

Collin hadn't given any thought to asking her out but when the opportunity had presented itself, he'd jumped in with both feet. He still wasn't sure how he was going to land. She'd been resistant, and he sensed her conflict had more to do with their work relationship than anything else. At least that was what he hoped. Although there were no hard and fast rules about employees fraternizing, he could argue that point if he needed. They were both dedicated to their professions and neither would do anything to jeopardize their careers. Business would come first and everything else would fall into place as necessary.

Thinking about London fueled his excitement even more. He really wanted to know her better. He imagined they had much in common, despite her previous assumption that he was spoiled and pampered. He had no doubts that she also fathomed he was a bit of a playboy, but he intended to squash that notion the first chance he could. Despite what many thought of him, Collin's experience with women was nominal in comparison to other young men his age. He wasn't a virgin, but he'd been finicky about the women he'd shared time and space with. In college, his mother's admonishments to be cautious and his father's warnings about everything that could go awry with the wrong partner had often rung loudly in his thoughts. To avoid the risks, he'd spent his energy on his studies, leaving the girls to everyone else.

But London Jacobs had him reevaluating all those life lessons. He was reassessing his priorities and playing daily games of what-if. He had often imagined what it must have been like when his mother had fallen in love. He'd been curious about his father's mind-set when Matthew Stallion had realized that she was his heart. Collin now found himself pondering if he, too, could ever have what they shared. For the first time, he was excited about the possibilities and didn't have a clue if the possibility existed with his new friend. But a Stallion could dream, he thought.

London suddenly calling his name broke through his thoughts. When he looked up she was moving toward him, an urgency in her step as she crossed the parking lot. She was stunningly beautiful, seeming like a category-five hurricane in a petite size-six frame. She moved swiftly on four-inch heels and everything about her was captivating. He felt his mouth pull into a wide grin as he lifted his hand and waved.

London felt like a high school cheerleader with a crush on the popular football player. She was practically giddy with excitement at the sight of Collin Stallion, and for the life of her she couldn't begin to fathom from where the flood of emotion had risen. She clenched her fists to stall the rise of anxiety and to resist the urge to throw herself at him so unabashedly. Because seeing him made her want to fling her body against his and hold on for dear life.

Collin Stallion was sheer perfection, she thought as she stared in his direction. He'd changed into a casual suit of polished sateen. It was expertly tailored with clean, modern lines and fitted him exceptionally well. The color was a rich deep burgundy and he wore a bright white T-shirt beneath it. He'd changed his shoes as well, a pair of pricey white Air Jordan sneakers now adorning his feet. He'd released his dreadlocks and the sun-kissed strands hung down his back past his broad shoulders. The thick tresses gave him a lionlike mane and he had the look of a regal emperor. He was too damn pretty and attracting a wealth of attention.

As their gazes locked and held, London felt her

cheeks heat with color. Something she didn't recognize pulsed deep in her feminine core and the look he was giving her seemed to tease every ounce of her sensibilities. His eyes were intoxicating, their color a rich amber with flecks of gold that shimmered beneath the setting sun. There was something behind his stare that was heated, igniting a wealth of ardor in the pit of her stomach.

"Collin, hey!" she exclaimed as she reached his side. "I apologize. I didn't mean to be late. I hope you haven't been waiting here long."

He shook his head. "You're fine. You're right on time. I was actually early."

London nodded, suddenly feeling completely out of sorts. She was beyond nervous, her knees beginning to quiver ever so slightly. She felt him sense the rise of discomfort, his own anxiousness dancing sweetly with hers.

He took a deep breath. "Why don't we go inside? I'm sure our table is ready for us," he said as he pressed a gentle hand against the small of her back.

A jolt of electricity shot through London's body at his touch, the intensity of it feeling like she'd combusted from the inside out. It took everything in her not to trip across the threshold of the restaurant's front door.

London couldn't stop laughing, tears rolling over her cheeks. She leaned back in her chair as she pressed both hands to her abdomen. Her face glowed, the light and laughter gushing like a beacon from her eyes.

"And that's how you took a walk on the wild side? You crashed your father's car?"

Collin was laughing as intensely. "I was fifteen! What did I know? And he wasn't my father then. But stealing his car was the best thing that ever happened to me," he said with a slight shrug of his shoulders.

"Are you honestly trying to tell me that there was a benefit to your criminal enterprise? What would have happened if he and your mother hadn't liked each other?"

"I think when you meet him you'll see that he still would have supported me. Dad's that kind of guy."

London smiled, settling back in the level of comfort they'd found with each other. She took a sip of her beverage. Everything about their evening filled her with joy. Conversation had been easy and entertaining. He loved to talk, and she was completely engaged in the stories he told about himself and his family. They'd debated politics, religion, books and the philosophy of education in America. He was slightly nerdy, liking Japanese anime and manga and the augmented reality game *Pokémon Go*. He was also a die-hard *Star Wars* fan, which gave him two thumbs-up on her checklist.

She couldn't remember the last time she'd had so much fun. The food had been on point, with Collin recommending his favorites. She'd taken his lead and had started with the tuna tartare and lobster bisque. For the entrée, she'd selected the prime rib eye topped with blue crab, shrimp and the most delectable béarnaise sauce. Now she was stuffed, and he was trying to ply her with dessert.

"I love their carrot cake. It's dense and topped with this caramel-and-nut topping. It's divine!" he exclaimed as he pursed his lips and blew a kiss into the air with the tips of his fingers. "However, I also know the chocolate mousse in the chocolate candy shell topped with the fresh whipped cream, straw-berries and mint is pretty darn good, too!"

"I could not eat another bite," she said, shaking her head emphatically. "You're going to have to roll me out of here as it is!"

Collin persisted. "How about we get it to go? You can enjoy it later when you're still thinking about me."

London laughed, "That's a bit presumptuous! What makes you think I'm going to give you a sec-ond thought later?"

He shifted forward in his seat, leaning in her direc-tion. The gesture felt conspiratorial and London found herself leaning toward him. "You're already giving me a second thought. Later, you'll be on thoughts five, six and seven. I have that effect on people."

"On people, or on women?"

Something mischievous twinkled in the stare he gave her. His eyes narrowed slightly, the intensity of his gaze sweeping a flood of heat through her. She reached for her wineglass and took a large gulp to cool the rise in her temperature. Collin didn't bother to respond, gesturing for their waiter instead. After ordering two slices of carrot cake to go, he focused his attention back on her.

"Thank you."

Her brow rose questioningly.

"For not canceling. I know you thought about not coming. But I'm glad you did. I've had a really good time."

London took a breath and held it for a split second.

"I did think about canceling. I wasn't sure this was a good idea."

"And now?"

"I'm still not sure. You're quite interesting, Collin Stallion."

"Interesting is a good thing."

"It can be."

"Can I be honest with you?"

She nodded. "I hope you wouldn't ever lie to me!"

"I find you intoxicating," he said, his voice dropping an octave. "You intrigue me, London, and I hope this won't be our last date. I would really like for us to get to know each other better."

There was a moment of pause as she pondered his statement. A slow smile pulled at her lips. "Who said this was a date?"

Collin laughed, "Did I forget to tell you that? My bad!"

The amusement in her eyes vanished, her laugh lines suddenly turning serious. "This has been great, but I don't want to give you the wrong impression," she started.

Collin interrupted her, holding up a hand to stall whatever else was on the tip of her tongue.

"London, I would never do anything to compromise our work relationship. I understand how important this job and your career are to you. As it is to me, and as my superior and mentor, I have great respect for you. I would just like us to continue to enjoy each other's company as we get to know each other. I have no expectations and you have been completely up-front with me, so there is nothing for me to misinterpret about our relationship. I just hope you'll take the opportunity to know me better. I believe you and I could be great friends."

London paused, completely smitten by the sweetness of his words. *The man is good*, she thought to herself. Aloud, she said, "I think we're already good friends, Collin. I just don't want you expecting more from me that I don't have to give. I'm very happy with my life the way it is. I'm not looking for a romantic relationship right now."

"That's good to know," he said, that look of mischief returning to his eyes. "I'm not looking for a romantic relationship either."

They sat and talked for another thirty minutes, chatting about everything and nothing. When the bill was paid, and their desserts boxed and bagged, Collin walked her back to her car. The late-night air had changed, a slight chill teasing a rainstorm.

"Thank you again," Collin said as he opened the car door and helped her into the driver's seat.

"Thank you, Collin. I had a wonderful time. I'll see you in the office tomorrow."

"Good night!"

As London closed the car door, Collin gave her a wave of his hand and took a step back. He stood watching as she turned the key to start the car. But nothing happened. Despite her persistent efforts, the engine would not crank. He met her gaze as she shot him a quick look out the driver's-side window, frustration beginning to furrow her brow.

He shook his head and reopened her door. "That doesn't sound good. Has it happened before?" he asked as he reached in and popped the lever for the hood.

London nodded, hating to admit that it had happened a few times and she'd been neglectful about taking the vehicle to be serviced. Usually, it only took a few tries, turning the key just so, before it started.

"Might be a bad battery," Collin said, his head lost beneath the hood as he shook wires and checked the connections at the battery terminals.

London peered at where he pointed. "It's not. The battery is brand-new and I've had it tested."

"Then it's something else electric. The starter may be damaged or a solenoid."

London wrapped her arms tightly around her torso. "This cannot be happening," she muttered under her breath.

"Don't stress," Collin said as he pushed a call button on his smartphone and pulled the device to his ear. He waited for it to be answered on the other end.

"Who are you calling..." she started.

Collin held up an index finger as he began to speak. "Hey, Aunt Mitch! I need your help," he said, pausing for a split second as the aunt he'd just called spoke. "My friend's car won't start. She doesn't think it's the battery. It's brand-new, but the engine won't turn over at all."

The aunt seemed to be asking questions.

Collin answered. "Just a repetitive clicking sound." He paused. "That's what I thought, too. Unfortunately, I don't have any tools here with me to be sure, though. Is it possible to get it towed to your garage, please? It's put her down here outside of Truluck's on McKinney Avenue." He paused again. "Thank you, Aunt Mitch. I really appreciate it. I'll drop by tomorrow and square up with you." There was another brief exchange between them before Collin disconnected the call and placed his cell phone back into his pocket.

"I could have called triple A."

"My uncle Mark's wife, Michelle, is one of the best auto mechanics in the business. She won't steer you wrong and I trust her implicitly."

"Well, thank you. I appreciate the referral. I think."

He smiled. "Why don't we gather up your personal belongings and move them to my car? My aunt says she'll look at the engine first thing in the morning and then call you about the repairs, so you'll know what you're looking at. As soon as the tow truck gets here I can give you a ride home."

London blew out a heavy sigh. "That's not necessary. I just need to arrange for a rental." She stole a quick glance toward her wristwatch, surprise painting her expression as she realized the late-night hour. She cussed. "I guess I'll have to call in the morning."

Amusement danced across his face. "Like I said, I'll give you a ride."

Minutes later, London was directing him to her Turtle Creek Boulevard home. He maneuvered his car left onto Olive Street, then merged onto the Dallas North Tollway. Exiting at Lover's Lane, he made the right turn onto Baltimore Drive and then another right toward their destination.

The midrise luxury condo was in the heart of Preston Hollow, with excellent views of downtown Dallas. She lived in the penthouse, the upscale residence offering two bedrooms and two and a half baths. It was an open floor plan that was great for entertaining. As Collin took in the high-end finishes, the granite countertops in the chef's kitchen, the designer appliances, custom cabinetry and marble floors, he was duly impressed. He was also still feeling the surprise of her inviting him up for a cocktail.

When they'd pulled into the building's parking lot he had offered to carry her things to her door for her. She'd resisted at first, and then, in the blink of an eye, she'd changed her mind, inviting him to her door and inside. There had been the briefest moment of hesitation and he sensed she was second-guessing her decision. Then, just like that, she seemed resolved with her choice, giving him a quick tour of her spacious floor plan.

He could feel her watching him as he took in her surroundings. There was no denying that he hoped to discover more about her now that he'd been welcomed into her home. Something in her demeanor hinted that not many men had ever had the privilege, so he was feeling particularly honored. He paused in front of the sofa table, admiring the framed photographs that adorned the top. He lifted one into his hands and stared at it. "You're an only child?"

"Yes! I am the brightest light in the lives of Lincoln and Patricia Jacobs, who have doted on me since the day I was conceived. They had just finished touring Westminster Abbey with some missionary church group when they sneaked off for some quality time together. Nine months later, they were blessed with me."

"And named you London for the memory?"

She giggled, "It's cheesy, I know!"

"Actually, I think it's very sweet."

"It really is. They're cute, my parents. Very down-to-earth. Very simple folk. I think you would like them and I'm fairly certain they would adore you!"

"I do have a way with parents," he said smugly.

London rolled her eyes skyward. "I just bet you do!"

He chuckled warmly, "I imagine Mom and Dad are very proud of you and your accomplishments."

"I think they'd be prouder if I were married with two or three kids. They're kind of old-fashioned that way."

Collin laughed, nodding his understanding.

She gestured for him to take a seat. "What would you like to drink? I have a fully stocked bar."

"Whatever you're drinking will be fine," he said, as he moved to the living room sofa.

She raised an eyebrow in thought as she stepped behind the wooden bar and filled two cognac glasses with Hennessy. She transferred the prized carrot cake from the box to two small plates. She gathered everything onto a tray and eased back to where he sat, settling on the cushioned seat beside him as she passed him a glass. "You're quite pleased with yourself, aren't you?"

"Excuse me?" he chuckled softly.

"You like to save people. It's that hero complex of yours. I imagine you're quite pleased right now. That you could come to the aid of a damsel in distress."

"Hero complex? Really?" Collin laughed. "You were hardly in a situation that you couldn't handle yourself. And I imagine that if I ever referred to you as a *damsel in distress*, you'd probably take my eye out!"

She laughed with him. "I'm glad you're getting to know me."

He took a sip of the cognac she'd given him, savoring the robust taste. They continued their conversation and ate cake, enjoying each other's company. He talked about being adopted by his father and having a baby brother. She shared that before her career in law she had wanted to be a painter and still dabbled in oils when the moment moved her. They talked about their jobs, the case and her five-year plan. He confessed to not being certain about his own future, still undecided about where he would eventually land in the legal game. Their talk wavered from serious to nonsensical and back. He made her laugh with his bad jokes and she amused him with her sarcasm. Each found the other engaging and delightful, and the ease with which they allowed themselves to be vulnerable in the moment surprised them both. They sat contentedly together for a good long while. She had turned on her stereo and someone's jazz echoed out of the speakers. Eventually they found comfort in the quiet, neither needing to speak. It felt like the most natural thing for them to do.

Neither was sure who fell asleep first. London had fallen against the sofa arm, her legs stretched outward. Collin had kicked off his shoes and was lying beside her. His back was pressed against the sofa cushions and his body was curled warmly around hers. One arm had fallen around her waist, holding her close, her buttocks pressed into his groin.

Neither would argue that she woke first, her eyes flitting back and forth as she gained her bearings. She had no sense of time and was dumbstruck to find Collin still there and the two of them wrapped so warmly around each other. His breathing was heavy, deep exhalations of air that would have been loud snores if he'd been able to move his body to another angle. She turned her body slowly, until she could face him, the oversize sofa offering just enough space for them both to lie easily side by side.

She stared, in awe of how peaceful he looked. His thick lashes fluttered effortlessly, what must have been sweet memories dancing in his dreams. There seemed to even be a faint smile pulling at his full lips. She pressed a hand to his chest. The muscle beneath the shirt he wore was solid, his taut flesh rock hard. She closed her eyes, leaning forward slightly to inhale the cologne that scented against his skin. It was a resolutely masculine scent reminiscent of a Mediterranean breeze. He smelled divine! London took another deep breath and held it, the rich fragrance lingering in her lungs.

When she opened her eyes again Collin was staring at her, his gaze flickering back and forth across her face. Desire rained from his gaze; the look he was giving her was simply intoxicating. Beneath her fingertips his heartbeat was racing, pulsing with a vengeance against her palm. Her lips lifted in the sweetest smile.

"I didn't mean to doze off," he said, his voice a low whisper.

London met the look he was giving her with one of her own. "I fell asleep, too," she whispered back.

"I've overstayed my welcome. I need to get up and get out of your hair."

A moment passed and neither made any effort to move, still gazing at each other, memorizing each fine line that detailed their expressions.

Collin's eyes flickered closed and then open. "I swear," he repeated. "I'm going."

She laughed, acutely aware of the urgent matter pressing tightly against the front of his slacks for attention. She shifted her body forward until she was pressed firmly against him. His arm tightened around her waist, his fingers gripping the back of her dress.

"You're not playing fair," he said. "You know what you're doing to me, right?" He pushed his pelvis forward, the gesture teasing.

"That feels like a personal problem to me."

"Oh, it's very personal. It's about as personal as you can get."

"I imagine that's why you haven't moved yet?"

"That and you need to move first. Unless you want me to roll over you?"

London giggled softly. She pushed her body even closer against his.

"London," he started, "maybe we should…"

"Maybe we should just stop talking," she said. She trailed her fingertips along the profile of his face. "In fact, I can think of a few other things we could be doing," she concluded, and then she kissed him, capturing his luscious lips with her own.

London couldn't begin to explain what had possessed her to kiss Collin. She had no words for the wealth of emotion that had suddenly consumed her, but the nearness of him had ignited a wave of heat that could have melted chocolate before rising rapidly until it could soften metal. His mouth was sheer perfection against her own. Full, plump pillows that cushioned hers so sweetly that she felt as if her lips were slow dancing against clouds. His mouth was inviting and his tongue responsive as she slipped her own past the line of his teeth to dance sweetly in the warm, wet cavity. The kiss was exhilarating, so spectacular that London knew it wouldn't be the last time she kissed the man.

Chapter 4

Every muscle in Collin's body had hardened with a ferocity he had never before known. It took every ounce of fortitude he possessed to keep from combusting, his core ready to explode like a volcanic eruption. The heat coursing through his midsection was so searing that he felt like his whole body was melting, moisture seeping from every pore. London was teasing him brazenly, her hands dancing in easy exploration across his body. It was becoming increasingly difficult to ignore her charms. She passed her palm across his manhood, trailing her fingers ever so slowly, and he jumped, the abrupt gesture unexpected.

Her lithe frame was tight and lean, her skin soft as silk. She came out of her clothes quickly, pulling her dress up and over her head. He was blessed with the sight of black lace, a pretty bra and panties adorning her slender lines. His touch was determined, large fingers softly kneading the tender flesh. His mouth was still dancing with hers, the kisses even sweeter and more passionate.

Collin pulled at her bra, exposing one bare grapefruit-sized breast and then the other. Her nipples were rock candy hard, dark protrusions that begged for his attention. His lips followed where his fingers led, his tongue lashing at the sweet confections like he was starved. He looked up, taking in her closed eyes and the moans of appreciation that encouraged his ministrations. He felt himself harden even more, if such a thing were possible.

Collin lifted himself up and over her, pulling at the black panties that separated him from what he desired. He sat upright up on his knees and pulled at his own clothes, snatching his shirt from his broad chest and flinging it to the floor. She leaned up, tugging at the belt around his waist. She pulled at his zipper until his pants were undone, pushing them down until they were rolled around his hips. He eased her back against the sofa, using his lips to push her slowly back against the cushions. With a fervor that surprised them both he snatched her lace panties from her body and teased his hands between her firm thighs. He felt her quiver with anticipation as he slid one finger and then another into her most private space. Her arousal scented the air, female anticipation like a beloved perfume. Moisture coated his fingers, her desire slick and abundant. His cock twitched and pulsed, reacting with a mind of its own.

He wanted her. He wanted her so badly, he imagined that his heart would shatter if she were to dismiss him before he were able to savor a taste of her nectar. He slid his hands down the backs of her legs, pushing her knees to her ears. He eased his way down the short length of her torso, kneeling before her most private garden as if he were in prayer. He appraised her, the vertical smile inviting him to touch and tease the delicate walls. He was emboldened, his hunger suddenly insatiable. He sank his face into her feminine bowl and pressed an intimate kiss against the treasure. He probed her gently with his tongue, then licked her from top to bottom. He lapped at her, his ministrations greedy, until she gasped and screamed, her hands pressed firmly against the back of his head.

Their sexual aerobics lasted well into the wee hours of the morning. They made love on the living room sofa, the floor, the kitchen counter, the dining room table and in the bathroom shower. When they finally made it to her bedroom and her bed, London was completely in awe of his prowess, unable to fathom how he was able to rise to each occasion so effortlessly. She was exhausted, her body feeling as if she'd run multiple marathons back-to-back. She was giddy, riding a sweet high that had her slightly delirious. Her body was nicely satiated, the sensual gratification having satisfied her physically and emotionally. She was feeling so good she didn't even fret over the fact she'd broken every one of her rules. Not only had she welcomed him into her home, but she'd opened herself to him, had thrived on the intimacy and was actually excited about him spending the night in her bed. She shook her head at the absurdity of it all as she cuddled closer against him, his body cradled nicely against hers. The warmth of his touch was comforting as Collin pressed

a damp kiss against her bare shoulder. He reached for
the cotton blankets and pulled the covers over them
both. London smiled as Collin began to snore softly,
then she, too, drifted off to sleep.

The water was running in the shower when London's alarm rang. For just the briefest moment she forgot that she wasn't alone, and her heart began to race,
something like fear piercing her midsection. Then she
remembered Collin had fallen asleep in her bed and
was obviously in her shower. She threw her legs off
the side of the bed, allowing her feet to rest against
the carpeted floor. Her eyes were drawn to the Rolex
watch on the nightstand. It was white gold, the styling
classic with its black dial and diamond bezel. She liked
that he felt comfortable enough to leave his personal
belongings lying casually about.

Looking around the room, she noticed he'd retrieved his clothes from the living room. They now
lay neatly folded over the wingback chair in the corner
of the room. He'd gathered up her clothes as well, the
black lace bra and panties resting against the chair's
seat cushion. His efforts were endearing, and she was
touched by the gesture.

Trusting a man didn't come easily for London. It
still surprised her that she'd opened herself so willfully to Collin Stallion, feeling as if she'd fallen headfirst into an abyss with no thought to the consequences
if things between them suddenly went left. Trusting
Collin contradicted everything she espoused. Despite
the comfort she felt with him, she still didn't know
him. Sex on a first date was unfathomable and yet, it
had been the most natural thing for her to do.

Being with Collin made her think of all her favorite things bundled into one magical moment. He was her mother's macaroni and cheese, summer vacation in the Hamptons, deepwater fishing with her daddy and a good romance read after a successful court win. He had butterflies flitting around in her tummy and she was giddy and light-headed around him. Everything she'd discovered about the man had her feeling as safe as being home with her own family, everything about his nature feeling strong and protective. She liked Collin more than she could have ever imagined, and although that surprised her, it also had her excited to see how their relationship might grow. She stood up and headed toward the bathroom.

Collin stood behind the glass door with his head tossed back over his shoulders, the spray of water raining down his broad chest and shoulders. He slowly twisted his neck from side to side and then he stuck his head beneath the flow, his eyes closed as the warm water washed over his face. His hands trailed the length of his torso as he lathered suds across his skin. She was completely enthralled as she stood staring at him.

He suddenly realized he was being watched, turning to meet her gaze. He winked and smiled. "Good morning!"

"Good morning!"

"I hope you don't mind. I figured it would be easier to shower here and just change clothes when I get back to my house."

London shook her head. "It's not a problem at all. As long as I can bum a ride into work with you."

He pushed open the glass door. "I guess we both need to make time, then. I can't be late. The woman I work with can be a bit of a stickler about punctuality."

"Really?" she said as she stepped into the enclosure with him.

"They say she's a beast. Personally, I haven't experienced that side of her, but I don't want to take any chances."

"Is that what they say?" London asked, her hands lightly grazing his back and buttocks.

Collin shook his head. "You're trying to start something," he muttered as she snaked her arm around his waist and gripped his manhood. She stroked him boldly as his erection sprang, full and abundant.

"I wouldn't do any such thing," she laughed, a hint of devilment in her tone.

"You're trying to get me in trouble on purpose."

"I'm thinking you won't have to worry about it. I'll just write you a note. I'm sure that beast you work with will excuse you being late this one time."

He suddenly spun around, scooping her up into his arms as he pressed her back against the tiled walls. One hand held her firmly, his fingers clutching her buttocks as she wrapped her legs around his waist. His other hand moved between them, slipping into the slick moistness between her legs. London gasped, surprise widening her eyes as he began to stroke her as boldly as she was just caressing him.

"I think you're the one starting something," she murmured, her breathing suddenly static.

"Oh, baby," he exclaimed. "You just don't know the half of it!"

* * *

That shower lasted a good thirty minutes longer than planned. When Collin pulled his car into the driveway of his home, his parents were standing on the porch, waving Jake off to school. The car pool driver tooted her horn and waved as she pulled off, passing him on her way out. Collin cussed.

"I was hoping to sneak in and out without being seen," he said as he tossed London a look.

"You live at home with your parents," she said smugly. "How were you planning to make that happen?"

"I live in the guesthouse with my own entrance and key. It's very private and I can come and go as I please," he said, his own tone slightly haughty.

London laughed, clearly amused. Collin rolled his eyes skyward, equally entertained by the turn of events.

Matthew and Katrina were eyeing them both curiously. His mother was holding a large mug of coffee in her hand, her eyes narrowed. Amusement danced across his father's face. The younger couple sat watching them both briefly as Collin weighed his options. When Katrina suddenly leaned to mumble something to her husband, London burst out laughing a second time.

"Your mother just realized you didn't come home last night. I think you might really be in trouble."

Collin gave her another look. Embarrassment flooded his face, coloring his cheeks a deep shade of red. London reached a warm hand out, laying it against his forearm. "You might as well go face the music. We need to get to the office, so you should go change."

"I am so sorry," he said, apologizing profusely.

London chuckled, "You don't need to apologize to me. I'm going to sit right here until you get back."

He opened his door and stepped out. "I don't think so," he said. "It's your fault we're late, so you're going to have to face the music with me."

He closed his door and moved around the back of the car to the passenger side. He pulled her door open and held out his hand. London's eyes widened as he laughed heartily. "I'm serious!" he said. "Let's move it!"

Before London could respond, Matthew called out to them. "Good morning!"

"Hey, Dad! Mom! Good morning," Collin said as he helped London out of the car, closing the door after her.

London muttered under her breath. "I am so going to make you pay for this!"

He pressed a hand against the small of her back and whispered back, "It's going to be fine. Just don't panic."

"You've got me doing the morning walk of shame and telling me not to panic."

Collin chuckled, "I never thought about it like that."

"Your mother is going to hate me!"

He laughed again. "My parents are going to love you," he said as he leaned to kiss her cheek. He entwined his fingers between hers and pulled her along. They climbed the short flight of steps to the front porch. "Good morning," he said again.

Matthew looked at his watch. "You're out and about early this morning."

Collin nodded. "London's car broke down last night and I had to help her get it towed to the garage for Aunt Mitch to look at. She needed a ride to work this morning, so I volunteered to give her a hand."

He gestured toward the young woman. "Mom, Dad, this is London Jacobs. London, this is my mother, Katrina Stallion, and my father, Matthew Stallion."

London extended her hand politely. "Mrs. Stallion, Mr. Stallion, it's a pleasure to meet you. Collin has told me so much about you both." She smiled sweetly.

Katrina was still clutching her coffee cup tightly. Her eyes skated across her son's face and back as she watched her husband shake hands with the young woman. She forced a smile to her face. "It's nice to meet you, London. Please, come inside. Would you like a cup of coffee?" she said as she turned abruptly. Her gaze narrowed as she gave Collin another look.

Matthew gestured for London to follow his wife and as he brought up the rear, he slapped his son against his back, the heavy-handed gesture accompanied by a bright smile.

London stood nervously in the foyer, her hands clutched tightly together in front of her. "Thank you for the offer," she said, "but I don't want to be any trouble."

"It's no trouble at all," Matthew said. "There's a full pot already brewed, and Katrina made blueberry muffins, as well. You're more than welcome to join us."

London looked toward Collin. Before either could respond, Katrina was peppering her with questions.

"So, how do you and Collin know each other? We

didn't know he was dating anyone. How long have you two been acquainted?"

Collin wrapped his arms around his mother's shoulders, hugging her warmly. "London and I work together," he said. "And we're just friends. Please, don't scare her!"

Matthew laughed. "Your mother's just excited to meet your new friend," he said.

Katrina's stare shifted from one to the other, her jaw tightening ever so slightly. She didn't bother to respond.

Collin shook his head. "I just need to grab some files I forgot," he said, the little white lie spilling from his mouth. "Then we need to get going. I've already taken longer than I planned." He turned toward London. "I'll only be a quick minute," he said as he excused himself, heading toward the back of the home and the guesthouse in the rear.

London smiled, her eyes shifting toward the matriarch, who was still eyeing her too closely. "You have a beautiful home," she said, hoping to ease the rise of apprehension that billowed between them.

Katrina nodded. "Thank you," she answered. "Please, come sit. Collin may take longer than a minute. Are you sure I can't get you some coffee?"

"I appreciate the offer, but I'm fine. Thank you."

"You may not remember," Matthew said, "but we met briefly a few years back when you were being honored by the Association of Black Women Attorneys. I was impressed by your accomplishments, Ms. Jacobs."

"Thank you, sir. And, please, call me London. I do remember. I was honored to hear you speak. We've met before as well, Judge Stallion. I participated in one of your clinics at the Girls Club when I was in high school. Your story was one of the reasons why I became an attorney."

Katrina smiled, a moment passing between the two women. "I've met so many girls since I started participating in that program. It makes me happy to know I've had an impact."

"You've been a wonderful influence on many of us."

Collin suddenly moved back into the room. He had changed into a black suit, gray dress shirt and matching necktie with black, gray and red stripes. Black leather loafers adorned his feet. At the sight of him a full grin pulled at London's lips, the wide smile filling her face. Collin grinned back, and the duo burst out laughing, seeming to share a secret only they were privy to.

Collin's parents exchanged a look. "You clean up nicely," his mother said, an air of sarcasm in her tone.

He moved to her side and eased his arms around her in a warm embrace. He kissed her cheek, then extended his arm to shake his father's hand. "We really have to run," he said.

London stood up, sauntering toward the door to meet him. "It was very nice to meet you both," she said again, looking toward his parents.

"We hope you'll visit again," Matthew said. "Maybe stay a little longer next time."

"You two have a good day," Katrina said, a little less enthusiasm in her tone.

London felt the woman's displeasure rising like morning mist and could only imagine what his mother had to be thinking about her. Collin grabbed her hand and pulled her along beside him.

The couple practically raced from the house. Hand in hand they descended the steps, giggling like grade-schoolers. It was only as Collin backed his car out of the parking space, tossing one last glance toward the family home, did he realize his mother was standing in the doorway, watching them both intently.

Chapter 5

Paula and Felicia both rushed into London's office minutes after her arrival. Their excitement was palpable. Across the room Collin was standing in conversation with Perry, the two discussing the likelihood of the Dallas Cowboys making it to the Super Bowl. Paula eased the office door closed, tossing a quick look over her shoulder before dropping down into one of the cushioned chairs in front of the oak desk.

"So, how was it?" Felicia gushed, her voice a loud whisper.

"How was what?" London looked up from the file she was reviewing, eyeing them both curiously.

"Your date, of course," Paula said, looking over her shoulder a second time.

"We had a very nice dinner," London said. Laughter flickered in her eyes. She was bemused by the interest that painted her friend's expressions. "I had a good time."

Felicia shook her head. "Nope. We want details. Who did what? Who said what? Leave nothing out!"

London laughed, "He made dinner reservations. I showed up. We ate the most amazing rib eye and shrimp. Talked, laughed and just got to know one another."

"So, why didn't you call us when you got in last night? At least to let us know you were safe."

London giggled, "I forgot. Sorry."

Paula's head shook slowly. Her gaze narrowed as she leaned forward in her seat. "No. You didn't forget. You never forget anything. You didn't call because your date never ended, did it?"

London rolled her eyes, a slight smirk pulling at her full lips. "Of course it ended!"

Felicia gasped. "You got you some! Look at you! You're glowing!" She jumped up excitedly, then pressed a hand over her mouth to stall the squeal that threatened to spill past her lips.

London laughed. "Shush!" she said. "Are you trying to get us all fired?"

"Was he good? He was good, wasn't he? I have so many questions!" Paula jabbered.

"We had a very nice time," London said. She sat back in her seat, folding her arms over her chest. "There is absolutely nothing else to tell!"

"Oh, I'm sure there is something to tell!" Paula quipped.

"He's got her sprung!" Felicia interjected. "She likes him! Just look at her!"

"She *really* likes him," Paula added, her eyes

locked on London's face, searching for just the faintest hint of agreement.

"You two need to get back to work," London concluded.

Her two friends exchanged a look, then turned their attention back to her. Paula waved her index finger at her BFF as she stood up on her very high heels. "Drinks. My house. Tonight. You're not getting off the hook that easy!"

London chuckled again. "Sorry. I can't make it. I have a date."

"See!" Paula exclaimed. "You are so wrong!"

"Girl, she's getting some! There is nothing at all wrong with that!" Felicia interjected.

Laughter rang warmly around the room. London waved a dismissive hand in their direction. "I'll say this, and don't you dare tell him I said it," she started, the other two pausing with bated breath for a hint of tea to be spilled. "Collin Stallion is pretty damn special," she concluded. "He's all that, the bag of chips, the cherry on top *and* Christmas in July."

"If it sounds too good to be true, it might be too good…" Felicia started, a sliver of concern in her tone.

London shook her head slowly from side to side. Her eyes were bright, shimmering with elation. "No," she said, "he is sheer perfection!"

Collin entered the county courthouse building through the rear door, the entrance for employees only. He eased his way down the short length of hallway to the county clerk's office. There was a party of sorts happening inside, people standing idly about with cups of fruit punch in hand. Trays of cookies and brownies rested against the high countertop and the energy in the room was euphoric.

Mrs. Nettie Banks waved a wrinkled hand, gesturing for him to come inside. She called his name from where she stood holding court on the other side of the room. "Attorney Stallion! You made it!"

Collin greeted the woman warmly. "I told you I wouldn't miss this for anything in the world," he said. "It's not often we get to celebrate someone's retirement after forty-five years of public service."

Mrs. Banks gave him a warm hug, reaching up to whisper in his ear. "You keep reminding people of my age and you and I are going to become bad friends!" she said teasingly.

Collin chuckled, "Mrs. Banks, now, you know you don't look a day over twenty-one!"

She tapped him against his arm. "That good-looking daddy of yours taught you well, sunshine!"

"I'm sure he'll be by before the day is out to say goodbye."

The older woman nodded. "Your mama was just here a few minutes ago. I think she said she was headed upstairs. Something about needing to catch up with one of the mediators before they disappeared."

"Thank you. I'll run up and see if I can find her before I leave."

"Get you something to eat, baby. We have plenty of food."

Collin leaned to give the woman another hug. "Thank you, Mrs. Banks. And thank you for everything you've done for me. I appreciate how you helped me learn the ropes around here."

"Baby, you are family. I've known your mama and

daddy since forever. There was no way I was going to let you flounder around here by your lonesome. This place is a challenge even for the more experienced attorneys. I just wish my friend Maxine could have been here to see you now that you're all grown-up and practicing law like your daddy. She would have been so proud of you."

Collin had known Mrs. Maxine Bright. She'd been another staple in the Dallas judicial system, ensuring the clerk's office ran smoothly. She'd died his sophomore year in college, while he'd been away at school. The two old women had been the best of friends. His parents still spoke fondly of the woman. Together, Mrs. Banks and Mrs. Bright had left an indelible impression on the legal community. He leaned to give the older woman a kiss on the cheek.

He smiled. "So, what's next for you? Anything exciting planned?"

"I'm leaving on a cruise to Alaska in two weeks. Then another to the Mediterranean after that. I never had any kids so it's just me and my husband, Gerald. We plan to cruise and travel until the good Lord calls us home."

"You're going to be missed, but I'm sure you'll have a great time. Take care of yourself, Mrs. Banks."

"You, too, baby! You, too!"

Collin and his mother bumped into each other on the landing between the first and second floors. He was headed up as she was making her way down. Katrina was only slightly surprised to see her son.

"Collin!"

"Mom, hey! Mrs. Banks said you were here."

"I closed a case earlier and just wanted to speak with Ms. Daly. What brings you here?"

"I promised Mrs. Banks I'd come say goodbye before she left."

There was an air of awkwardness that wafted between them. Collin sensed something on his mother's mind and he knew what that was without her having to tell him.

"You're mad at me."

Katrina shook her head. "Not mad. Not mad at all. But I am a little disappointed."

"Why?"

"Because we didn't raise you to be so casual about your romantic relationships, Collin. Since you didn't come home last night I can only assume you spent the night at Ms. Jacobs's."

"Are you asking me?"

"Well, did you?"

Collin took a deep breath. "Please, don't do that."

"Do what? I just asked you a question."

"Please, don't treat me like I'm still twelve. I'm almost twenty-seven years old and you still treat me like a child."

"That is not true."

"It is, Mom. Not only do you treat me like a child, but sometimes I think you don't trust that you did raise me right. You keep waiting for me to make a mistake and do something stupid, so you can sweep in to fix it. But I don't need you to fix anything for me. I'm *not* a child anymore."

Katrina took a deep breath. She and her son stood staring at each for a quick few minutes. "I'm sorry," she said. "I never intended for you to feel that way. I just worry about you. I don't want you to get hurt and I don't want you to be taken advantage of."

"Just trust me, please."

"I do trust you. But I'm not okay with you sleeping around. Your father and I have both discussed with you the ramifications of you having casual sex with no regard for yourself or your partners. I will never support you hopping from one woman's bed to another. Never!"

Collin chuckled, "I'm not sleeping around, Mom."

"You know it's quite inappropriate for you to be in a relationship with someone you work with, right? Especially since you're just beginning to build your career."

"I have every intention of following the example you and Dad set. I'm sure there were plenty of people who thought your relationship was inappropriate and look how it worked out for you."

"Those were very different circumstances, Collin." His mother gave him a slight eye roll, crossing her arms over her chest. "You're trying to compare apples to oranges."

"I'm trying to point out that you and Dad knew when it was right for you. You fell in love and you didn't let anything deter you from having the relationship you have today. I can only hope to be half as happy as you two are."

Katrina brushed a hand down the front of her son's suit jacket. "And you think Ms. Jacobs is the one for you? Collin, you barely know her!"

"You're right. I don't know her. What I do know is that I want the opportunity to get to know her better without worrying that you won't support me."

"I will always support you, son. Even if I don't always agree with your methods. Just make sure you protect yourself, please!"

Collin grinned and wrapped his mother in a deep bear hug. His cheeks were flushed with excitement. "London is an amazing girl, Mom! I really think you're going to like her."

Katrina blew a soft sigh as she hugged her son back. "I'm sure she's very nice."

Collin gushed. "She's more than that! She's incredible. London Jacobs is everything!"

When Collin walked into the headquarters of Stallion Enterprises he had no doubts his mother had already called his father to share their discussion. He also knew with a fair degree of certainty that he was sure to get a lecture. He stole a quick glance at his watch, cognizant of the time. He had just under an hour before he was to meet London—they'd planned earlier to catch a movie and dinner. His day had been long, but he knew hers had been longer and he wanted to give her a bit of a reprieve. She'd been in court for most of the afternoon and court had a way of wearing a person down. Just a few hours could easily feel like a lifetime if things weren't going well for all involved.

He rode the elevator to the twelfth floor and took a left and then a right to reach the legal department. His father ruled from the large corner office that faced downtown Dallas. The prominent views of the city were breathtaking, and Collin had marveled at the magnificence of it since he was a boy. He'd promised himself once that one day he, too, would have what his father had. And it was about respect, more than the fame and wealth. Because his father was highly respected in the community.

In the beginning, it had taken them a hot minute to find balance with each other. Collin had been the stepchild of bad horror movies: disagreeable, angry and filled with teenage angst. Resistant to change, he hadn't been amenable to his mother's new relationship and he had taken every opportunity to let them both know. But Matthew's devotion to him and his mother had been the catalyst to a lifelong friendship that Collin trusted and valued. Now all he wanted was to make his father, and his mother, proud.

His father's secretary ushered him inside, and his dad greeted him warmly. "Somehow, I knew I'd be seeing you, son!"

"Hey, Pop!" Collin said in greeting as he dropped into a chair. "I had a few minutes and figured I'd stop by."

"Oh. I thought this might have something to do with your mother calling me about your new girlfriend."

Collin laughed, "That didn't take long!"

"You know your mother!"

The young man shook his head. "I really didn't mean to upset Mom. I was hoping not to run into you two this morning."

"Your mom was going to be upset no matter how she found out. It's just her nature and you're still her baby."

"But I'm not a baby!"

"I know that. So does she. But you need to understand that for more years than not, your mother was a single parent and you were her sole responsibility. She didn't coddle you but she was slightly overprotective. Now that you're grown, she's having a hard time letting go. But she loves you and she only wants the very best for you."

Collin blew a heavy sigh, a gust of warm breath blowing over his full lips. "So, what do I do, Dad?"

"I think you've already taken the first step. You and your mother talked. She knows how you feel. Now, you just keep talking. Answer her concerns in a respectful way but stand your ground. This is your life and you have to live it your way. But let her share in your joy. If this young lady makes you happy, let your mom see that. Don't keep it a secret. Bring Ms. Jacobs around every now and again so we can get to know her, too. Because all we have ever wanted for you is for you to be happy."

Collin nodded as his father continued.

"And stop sneaking around like you have something to hide. If Ms. Jacobs is as special as you claim, then she deserves better from you."

"I wasn't…"

"You were. If you're spending your nights with this young woman, just show us the courtesy of letting us know that you won't be home, so we don't worry. And don't sneak her into or out of the guesthouse."

Collin rolled his eyes. "It was just one night!" he muttered.

"So, you're saying there won't be any more?"

"I'm saying that I'm still trying to figure it out and I just need some privacy and some time to do that."

"That's fair. Just be mindful of everyone's feelings and respectful of all concerned. That's all I ask."

"Was it this hard when you started dating Mom?"

Matthew laughed, "It was challenging because we didn't want to do anything to compromise what we knew you needed. It was important to us both that we be an example to you of what a relationship should be and how you saw your mother when she did invite me into your lives. Now, your uncles were a complete and total pain in the ass! But they just did what family does when they care about you. What we will do to you, I'm sure!"

Collin grinned. "Mom's always telling people what a romantic you are and how you blew her away with your first date."

Matthew grinned. "I rented out the entire Dallas Cowboys Stadium. It was epic!"

"So, I should try something like that?"

His father laughed heartily, "I had deep pockets. Your pay grade is nowhere near there yet. You must do what works for you and your budget. Share with her what you enjoy. That will impress her more than anything. I'm sure your mother will also tell you that her favorite dates were those where we just sat and talked over coffee or read a book together."

"London and I are going to a movie and dinner later."

"What do you plan to see?"

"I thought I'd let her pick the film."

His father nodded. "Well, just have fun. That's most important."

"I know you have a meeting to get to so I'm going to get out of your way. I might run by Uncle Mark's office to see what he's up to. Maybe get some advice from him, too." Collin stood up, his father rising onto his feet, as well.

"I'm sure your uncle Mark has plenty of advice to

give. Before he married your aunt Mitch he considered himself quite the Romeo with the ladies! You might be better served to go talk to your uncle John."

Collin grinned. "I might go see them both, then!"

"Just remember, you can get all the advice in the world, but you still need to follow your own instincts. Do what feels right for you."

"Thanks, Dad."

"I love you, son."

"I love you, too, Pop." Collin paused at the door, turning to give his father a look, his grin canyon-wide across his face. "Just in case, I probably won't be home tonight."

Matthew chuckled, "I'll let your mother know," he said.

Chapter 6

The sun was just beginning to set when London left her office. She was debating whether to catch the bus or call for an Uber when she saw Collin standing in front of her car. He was leaning against the trunk, his ankles and arms crossed as he waited. When he saw her, he smiled as he waved her car keys around his index finger. Her whole face lifted with glee as she waved a hand in his direction, practically skipping to his side.

"Hey there! You picked up my car!"

"I did and it's running like a charm. Your starter was bad, so my aunt replaced it. She also changed your oil and did a maintenance check. She said you need to start thinking about new tires. You only have a few thousand miles left on the treads."

"Thank you. What do I owe her?"

"You don't owe her anything at all. It's been handled."

"I don't want you paying my bills, Collin."

"No need for you to worry about that. I hadn't planned on paying your bills. But I did pay for the arrangements I made."

"That's really not…"

"Please, don't give me an argument, London. It was the least I could do."

London stared at him. There was a moment of hesitation where she bit back the impulse to say something snarky. But there was something in the look he was giving her that seemed to snatch the words, and the emotion, from her. "I missed you," she said instead. "How was your afternoon?"

"Long," he said as he passed her keys to her. "I ran into my mother down at the courthouse."

London moved to the driver's-side door, disengaging the door locks. She watched him as he sauntered to the passenger side and pulled open the door. "Your mother hates me, doesn't she?" she asked as she slid into the driver's seat.

Collin closed the car door and pulled at the seat belt. "No, she doesn't. My mother would like to get to know you."

"She said that?"

"She said a lot of things but nothing she said was derogatory toward you."

"You're a bit of a mama's boy, aren't you?"

Collin laughed, "You say that like it's a bad thing."

"So, you admit it."

There was a flicker in his gaze that London found intriguing as she eyed him intently.

"My mother was the first woman I fell in love with," he said, his tone dropping to a loud whisper. "I measure every woman who has come into my life since against her. She has set a very high bar for any future Mrs. Stallion. There isn't anything I wouldn't do for my mother because I know what she sacrificed to raise me after my biological father died. I know she had to make some hard decisions over the years and I appreciate every opportunity she's been able to afford me. I want her to be proud of me and I will do whatever I need to ensure she is. So, yeah, if that makes me a bit of a mama's boy, I'll own it."

London cut an eye in his direction. "One day I hope I have a son who loves me as much as you love her." She started the engine and pulled the car out of the parking spot and into ongoing traffic.

Neither spoke as London made her way toward her home. She reached for the radio and pushed the on button. Sam Hunt was singing the hook to his latest song. She began to bob her head in time to the music. When she broke out singing along Collin couldn't keep his amusement off his face. She knew all the words to the next four songs as well, joining in with Blake Shelton, Sugarland and Darius Rucker. She had a beautiful voice, her tone like thick molasses and warm red wine.

"I would never have taken you for a country music fan," he said.

"What did you take me for?"

"Hard-core rap, maybe even hard metal."

London laughed, "Well, I happen to love country music. I love the storytelling aspect of each song. They make me feel good. So, what do you like to listen to?"

"I'm not a fan of any one genre. I just love music. Country, reggae, classical, everything!"

"You probably don't have a favorite ice cream either."

"That's not true. Black cherry is my go-to flavor every time."

"Interesting."

"Why interesting?"

"I would have pegged you for chocolate, all day, every day!"

"Nope. Black cherry."

"Then you probably like those chocolate-covered cherries that come out every year around Christmas."

"I do. But I don't like the cherry. Just the juice and the flavor, so I suck the chocolate and cream off the cherries and then I spit them out."

"So, you eat the cherries in black cherry ice cream but not the cherries in candy?"

"They taste funny."

She eyed him with a raised brow.

"I'm finicky about my food," he said, his tone slightly defensive.

"You are so funny!" London exclaimed.

"Like you don't have any food fetishes."

"I don't. I just like good food. The only thing I don't eat is cottage cheese. Cottage cheese is nasty!"

"I like it with pineapple."

"Well, you can have it." She made a face and Collin laughed.

Her gaze flitted from the road to his face and back. She took a deep breath. "While we're on the subject…" she started. "I think it's important that you know I don't jump into bed with just anyone. I don't make it a habit to have sex with a man on the first date. I don't want you getting the wrong idea about me. What happened between us was highly unusual."

Collin shifted in his seat, his eyes blinking as he seemed to be pondering something. "How does the subject of ice cream and cottage cheese translate to sex? Please, explain that to me."

"Excuse me?"

"You said, 'while we're on the subject.' We were talking about food."

London grinned. "It made sense in that moment. I saw the segue and I took it. I just needed to make it clear that I'm not easy." She bit down against her bottom lip.

"Oh, I definitely didn't get *easy* from you! I appreciated that you were that into me. That you recognized just what a great catch I am, and you liked what I had to offer. That you liked me. *Really* liked me!"

London grinned. "You are slightly full of yourself, aren't you?"

Collin laughed with her. As they sat paused at the stoplight he leaned to kiss her, noting the heat that had risen to her cheeks, their color a warm shade of red.

"I'm full of you is what I am," he said. "And I don't think badly of you, if that's what you're worried about. What happened between us was a mutual decision. I wanted you as much as you wanted me."

Relief seemed to wash over her. "I didn't want to give you any mixed signals. We'd already talked about not wanting a romantic relationship and then we were sleeping together."

"London, I really like you. I would like us to see where we might be able to take this, but it's important to me that you are comfortable with whatever happens. If you want, we can put the brakes on and take a step back. I'll follow your lead. We don't ever have to make love again."

London shot him a look, narrowing her gaze on him. She'd pulled into the parking lot in front of her building and shut down the car's engine. "Well, that's not going to happen," she said emphatically.

He blew a heavy breath into the air, swiping a hand across his brow. "Whew! That's good to hear. You had me nervous for a second."

"So, you really didn't mean what you just said?"

"Oh, I meant it. I just had my fingers crossed that you wouldn't agree! It would break my heart if I couldn't make love to you again. In fact—" his voice dropped an octave "—I've been fantasizing all day about waking up in the mornings, tasting you."

London felt her face flush with heat, a current of electricity shooting like an arrow through her feminine spirit. She got a flashback of his head between her legs, her fingers twisted around his dreadlocks as his tongue lapped at her juices. She took a breath and cleared her throat. "For the time being, can we just say we're friends with benefits and leave it at that? Because I really enjoy making love with you, too, and I don't see any reason for us to fix what isn't broken."

"So, you just want me for my body?"

She rolled her eyes skyward. "For now, yes! You good with that?"

Collin stared into her eyes, his gaze dancing sweetly over her face. He pressed his lips to hers in a quick kiss and then he answered. "For now."

* * *

Side by side, Collin and London juggled a tub of buttered popcorn, two large carbonated beverages and four boxes of movie theater candy—M&M's, Twizzlers, Junior Mints, and Mike and Ike tropical-flavored chews. They were laughing hysterically as they navigated the twelve-screen movie theater to the fifth theater on the left and the comedy London had selected.

"Tell me, again, why you chose seats all the way in the back, in the corner?" Collin asked as he followed the beautiful woman up the flight of stairs to the reclining leather chairs they'd purchased online.

"Trust me," she said. "These are the best seats in the house." She lifted the center arm of the two adjacent seats so they could sit together with no obstruction. Minutes after they were settled comfortably against each other, the theater lights dimmed. London reached into the oversize tote bag she carried and pulled out a plush cotton lap blanket.

"You come prepared," Collin said as he reclined his seat until his legs were extended and his back was tilted comfortably for optimal view of the big screen. He wrapped an arm around the back of the chair and draped it over her shoulders.

As London leaned against him, nestling herself comfortably against his side, she pulled the blanket across their laps. "The theater gets cold," she said. "I hate being cold."

Collin pressed a damp kiss to her forehead. "Then we don't want you cold," he said.

After ten minutes of previews, the feature film started. The theater was almost empty, save for the two people who sat rows below them. London laid her head on Collin's chest, her own legs extended beside his. When he laughed his chest heaved up and down against her cheek and the heat from his body was deliriously sweet. She trailed her fingers down the length of buttons on his dress shirt, then rested her palm against his abdomen. Not quite a six-pack but darn close. His muscles were taut and firm beneath her fingertips.

Collin drew a large hand down the length of her back. His touch was heated and when his fingers paused just above the curve of her backside, her breath hitched in her chest. When he palmed the round of her buttocks, first one cheek and then the other, her pulse began to race, her heartbeat like a drumline in her chest. London shifted herself closer against him, easing one leg over his. She jostled the bucket of popcorn that rested in his lap, spilling some over the sides. As Collin moved the container to the empty chair on his left, she brushed at the kernels of popcorn that had spilled. Her fingers grazed his slacks and stirred the rise of nature beginning to press for attention. He reached down to pull that blanket higher, the cotton throw having shifted down toward his knees.

Both pretended to focus back on the movie, but their attention was solidly on the other. Heavy caresses teased flesh as Collin slipped his hand beneath her cotton top, gently massaging her soft skin. London closed her eyes and savored the sweet sensations he was inciting from her body. She traced a line along the length of his thigh, up and then down, and back again, over and over. Slow, methodic strokes that soon had him rock hard and wanting.

Laughter rang out loudly from the other patrons, something on the screen evoking gut-deep chortles. London laughed, too, as she slid her body up and over his, pressing her pelvis against the protrusion of muscle that had blossomed nicely. Beneath the cover of darkness, she began to grind against him, an erotic side-to-side shuffle. Collin's entire body tensed with pleasure as he pressed his hands to her hips and guided her movements.

London began to pant softly. She leaned her head forward, pressing her face into his neck. She dragged her tongue over his Adam's apple, licking the salt and the sweet from his skin. He tasted divine and she was hungry for more. He nudged her with his cheek, seeking out her lips. He kissed her, his mouth possessive as his tongue snaked past the line of her teeth to dance in the wet nook. Her hands cupped his face, her mouth moving voraciously over his. His hands still clutched her ass as he pushed his hips into her, matching her rhythm with his own.

Her orgasm began to build, the most delicious sensations sweeping through her. Collin struggled to contain his own. He pulled his mouth from hers to whisper in her ear. "I need to be inside you!" he gasped. "Or I'm going to pop right here in my pants."

London gasped. "We can't…can't have that happen," she panted, still rubbing her body against him. "I just… I just need…one more…one more minute…" And then she erupted, her body convulsing with an intensity that surprised her. Wave upon wave of unbridled pleasure fired from her nerve endings. She bit down against her bottom lip to keep from crying out as her orgasm dampened her lace panties. It was sheer bliss and he let her ride it out, wave after wave pushing her intensely against him.

They left the theater abruptly, candy and popcorn abandoned where they rested. They practically raced down the stairs, through the lobby and out the door. Collin pulled her anxiously by the hand to the car, her laughter ringing sweetly through the late-night air. The ride back to London's apartment was fraught with sexual energy. Despite his best efforts Collin couldn't resist stroking himself as she maneuvered the car through downtown Dallas. One hand was lost down the front of his slacks, stroking the length of his manhood, as the other played in the length of her natural hair, the curly strands entwined around his fingers.

In the elevator to the penthouse apartment her hands replaced his, gently kneading the fullness of his erection. The warmth of her palms felt exhilarating, the length of each finger clasping him firmly. He was nicely engorged, and both knew it would take very little to bring him to climax. Their kisses were passionate, deep and tongues entwined. Lips sliding like silk against satin in their own private erotic dance.

Before the door was locked behind them he was stepping out of his pants as they tore at each other's clothes. They were an amalgamation of arms and legs and mouths moving with desperate intensity. London dug into the bottom of her purse, finding a condom lodged in the corner of the lining. Tearing at the wrapper with her teeth she sheathed him quickly as he dropped to the carpeted floor and rolled onto his back.

London straddled him a second time, plunging herself down against him. His member was like a piston, plunging up and down, and then he arched his back as he thrust himself into her, the last of his energy exploding with a vengeance.

London lay sprawled on her back, staring up toward the ceiling. Collin lay in the bed beside her. They were holding hands, fingers locked tightly together. Neither had any idea of the time as they lay talking.

"I remember the first time I voted. You couldn't tell me anything. I strutted into that booth like I was the king of the walk. Then I stood there for ten minutes because I didn't have a clue what I was supposed to do after I ticked all the right boxes."

London laughed, "You kill me! You are so funny! I know you knew what to do."

"Trust me. I was completely lost."

"Well, I wasn't. I've been working at the polling sites as a volunteer since I was old enough to be accepted. I work voter registration drives, stuff party envelopes, whatever I can to help with the voting process. I was a champ the first time I voted! Swept in, made my voice heard and bam!"

The exuberance in her voice made Collin laugh. He squeezed her fingers.

She continued, "I do a lot of volunteer work. When the holidays get here, you're going to have to work with me down at the homeless shelter."

"I look forward to it. I've got a mission trip scheduled later in the year. Maybe you can join me? I work with a church youth group and we'll be building homes in Haiti."

"I would really like that!"

"Then let's definitely plan on it. I'll get you the details."

London slowly drew circles in the palm of his hand as a blanket of silence billowed between them. She took a deep breath. "I'm surprised that I like you as much as I do, Collin. You just keep surprising me."

Collin laughed, "Why is that?"

"I don't know," she said, shifting her body so that she was facing him. "Most men turn out to be a disappointment after the first few dates. But not you."

"I'll take that as a compliment."

"It was meant to be."

"Is that why you're not interested in a romantic relationship? Because you're afraid of being disappointed?"

"It's more than that. I just…" She paused, falling back against the mattress to stare back up at the ceiling.

Collin shifted onto his side, propping his head on his hand and elbow as he stared down at her. His brow was raised in curiosity.

London gave him a look before she continued. "The only man I was ever in a serious relationship with turned out to be a monster. He had this public persona that let you believe he was good and decent but behind closed doors he was the complete opposite."

"How long were you together?"

She took a deep inhale of air, holding the oxygen in her lungs for a brief moment. "Two years. He was a visiting law professor when I was in school. He was older, established, prominent in the community. I was completely enamored. We were engaged to be married and then…well…" She hesitated. "It just didn't work out," she concluded.

The expression that washed over her face gave Collin pause. Clearly, the memories were a source of consternation for her. Something about her ex and their relationship had left an indelible stain on her heart. She'd built a wall around herself, determined to shield her emotions. He understood that she was being protective, her defenses miles high. She was only so forthcoming with information, so he didn't push the issue. Instead, he traced the line of her profile with his index finger and changed the subject.

"I've had my heart broken twice," he said.

"You've been in love twice?" London laughed. "Just how young were you?"

"I was twelve the first time. Candice Baker was my reading partner and she promised to give me a kiss if I did her book report. It was on *The Hobbit* by J.R.R. Tolkien and I even read the whole book! And that thing was like three hundred pages! Then I wrote the best damn book report for her. She got an A!"

"And you didn't get your kiss."

"Nope. She left me hanging. She kissed my friend Michael instead because he lied and told her he was going to take her to Six Flags."

London laughed, "And the second time?"

"Now, that really hurt! I was seventeen and Lisa Wiles was my first real girlfriend. I gave her my virginity. We had big plans. After college we were going to get married, have kids, the whole nine yards. She went to school at Spelman and our freshman year she left me a voice mail message to say she couldn't do a long-distance relationship. She'd met someone at Morehouse and didn't want to have anything more to do with me."

"Ouch!"

"*Ouch* is right. She broke my heart."

"And since then?"

"Since then I've dated, but nothing serious. Not until now."

She rolled her eyes. "I thought we agreed we weren't looking for a relationship. We said we would be friends with benefits but that's all."

"That's a serious undertaking. Woman, you have been wearing my body out!"

"Me!"

"I haven't been giving my benefits to anyone else."

London laughed. "You are so stupid!" she said teasingly.

Collin's smile lifted in an easy bend, his bright smile lighting up the room. "I like you, too, London. I enjoy every minute we spend together. I can't imagine myself giving anyone else my benefits and it's important you know that. As we continue to get to know each other I hope you'll be open to whatever might happen between us."

"Like what?"

"Like redefining our relationship when it feels right, and you feel comfortable doing so."

"You think I'm crazy, don't you?"

"I think whatever has happened in the past has made you guarded and that's okay. I'm a very patient man."

"So, you're saying you really want a relationship, with the titles and the responsibility and everything that being a couple requires?"

"I'm saying that as we continue to get to know each other I hope that you will remain open to the possibility of our being more than friends."

"So, you want more than just the great sex?"

"Don't you? Not that I'm dismissing the great sex because I thoroughly enjoy what we share. I love making love to you. But whether you're willing to admit it or not, there's already so much more between us. Personally, I like that, and I don't want to lose it."

Collin watched her as she dropped into thought, contemplating his statement. Her eyes were closed, and it felt as if she were pondering every one of life's mysteries. Time seemed to be ticking slowly, as both were suddenly lost in their own feelings. London opened her eyes, turning her head ever so slightly to stare at him. Their gazes locked and in that moment, something between them shifted. Something both sensed, and neither was ready to express.

London gave him the sweetest smile, a wealth of joy shimmering in her eyes. "So, for now, can we just say we're *best* friends with privileges?"

Collin laughed, the wealth of it rising from deep in his midsection. "For now!"

As she reached out, he leaned to kiss her lips. She wrapped her arms around him and pulled him to her. His body sheltered hers as he eased himself above her. Their loving was slow and steady, a gentle melding of his body and hers until it was impossible to know where one stopped and the other started. It was golden and intoxicating, a thing of sheer bliss. Collin loved her like it was the first time and London held on to him as if her life depended on it. It was gratification that seared deep into the core of their spirits and made it impossible for either to ever turn back.

Chapter 7

London rolled to the opposite side of the bed, stretching her body out against the cold sheets. Collin had risen sometime in the wee hours of the morning, kissed her goodbye and left her. Now she was missing him something fierce and none of it made an ounce of sense to her. She hated that everything seemed to be happening so fast. Faster than she was able to control. And London hated not having control.

But there was something about Collin that had her wanting more and she had never wanted more from any man. Collin had a kind, gentle spirit. He was grounded in his faith and he stood for everything that was right in the world. Despite his sometimes quiet demeanor and laidback personality, there was a spirit about him, an energy that others fed on. He had drive and a determination that spoke volumes. He

Deborah Fletcher Mello   111

was headed for bigger and better and everyone who met him could see it.

London blew a soft sigh. Despite Collin's best efforts to put her at ease and engage her, she hadn't been able to tell him about her past. Not all of it. Not those things that had hurt her the most and still haunted her memories. She hadn't been ready to share everything. Some things were better left unsaid and buried. The nightmare of her past relationship wasn't something she cared to dig up and breathe life back into. That had been a hurt she would never wish on her worst enemy.

But it was important to her to be as open as she could be with Collin. She didn't want to hold back or have secrets between them. He deserved the best of herself that she could offer and for the first time in a very long while, she was willing to let her guard down and let a man in. Let him in. Most especially since she'd welcomed him so readily into her bed.

Her alarm clock sounded just as she threw her legs off the side of the bed and stood up. She'd only taken three steps toward the bathroom when her phone rang. The dedicated chime had her shaking her head. Patricia Jacobs calling so early in the morning meant a lecture was coming and for the life of her London had no idea what she'd done or how to prepare herself for what was surely coming. She answered the call on the fifth ring.

"Good morning!"

"Good morning, baby! You aren't still in bed, are you?"

"No, ma'am. I was just about to step into the shower. What's got you up so early in the morning?"

"Your daddy has a doctor's appointment. You know

how he is. Had to be the first one through the door. That man has truly started to work my last nerve lately."

London smiled into the receiver. Her parents were celebrating some forty-plus years of marriage, and nothing about their relationship surprised her. To her, they felt like the last of a dying breed, having married young, weathered more than their fair share of storms and still standing firmly on the love they had for each other. Deep down, London hoped to have that for herself someday, but no one wanted it for her more than her mother.

"I was hoping I could persuade you to come to church on Sunday."

"Church?"

"London Jacobs, don't act like I'm speaking a foreign language. You know darn well what church is!"

London laughed, "No, the question just surprised me. It's been a while since I last went to service."

"That's because you always have an excuse! Either this week isn't a good week or you have to work, or you have plans out of town. It's been excuse after excuse after excuse."

"I haven't been that bad."

"Yes, you have."

"Well, I promise to do better," London answered, knowing her mother was right and not wanting to admit it.

"Service starts at eleven o'clock and this Sunday I'm being honored. I was selected Woman of the Year. So, start by doing better this Sunday."

"That's great news, Mom! Congratulations!"

"It's not a big deal but I would like to have all my

family there to support me. Especially my wayward daughter that I'm always talking about, whom my church family barely remembers."

"So, you actually called to guilt me into coming to church with you on Sunday."

"It was either that or let your father call and order you to come. Which I will resort to if necessary."

London laughed, "No, don't do that. I'll be there."

"Wonderful! I hope Sister Hinton's sons are there. The oldest is a doctor and I'm not sure what business the youngest is in but he owns his own home."

"You're really planning to torture me like that?"

"It's not torture to introduce you to prospective partners, London. You really need to think about your future. Don't you want a family? A husband and children?"

"What I don't want is to have this conversation. I have to get ready for work." Annoyance shaded London's tone and she struggled to keep the attitude from her voice. "I'll call you later, okay?"

"That's fine. You know your daddy and I just want the best for you, right, London?"

"I do. It's fine. I'm fine. Don't worry about it."

"Well, I'm going to worry. It's what I do."

There was a moment's pause before London responded, "Would it be okay if I brought a friend with me on Sunday?"

"Bring both the girls! They've planned lunch after service and you know I'll have plenty of food here at the house."

"I'm not talking about Paula or Felicia. This is a new friend. Someone I just recently met."

"Well, you know any friend of yours is welcome anytime."

"Thank you. Then we'll see you and Daddy on Sunday, Mom. I love you."

"I love you, too, baby!"

Disconnecting the call, London sighed, a heavy gust of air blowing past her lips. Once again, her mother wanted her to meet someone's son, whom she hoped would be the one. For a brief second London thought about canceling at the last minute, making up some excuse not to show. And then she changed her mind. If she could convince Collin to join her, she would bring him home to meet her parents. Maybe then they'd be happy she had a man and she'd be more open to the possibility that maybe, just maybe, she had found the one.

"Collin!" Jake shouted and waved excitedly as his big brother came through the door.

Their mother was standing at the kitchen stove, flipping pancakes. Their father sipped coffee as he perused through the pages of *Forbes* magazine. Collin didn't miss the look the two exchanged as he entered the room.

"Yo, dude! What's up? Where you been?" Jake questioned as he and Collin slapped palms.

Collin grinned, amused by Jake's exuberance. "I've been working, dude! Doing that grown-up thing!"

"Bummer!" Jake exclaimed as he turned back to the food on his plate.

Collin leaned to kiss his mother's cheek as he passed by her. "Good morning," he said.

Katrina nodded. "Good morning. Are you on your way out, or are you sneaking back in again?"

Matthew laughed, lifting his gaze to give his wife and son a look.

Collin's smile was slightly goofy as he met the look she was giving him. "I'm headed to the office. I was hoping I might get a cup of coffee and maybe a few slices of bacon."

There was a moment that passed between them as his mother seemed to be considering his request. "Do you want pancakes, too?" she finally asked.

He nodded. "Yes, ma'am. Thank you."

He moved to the kitchen table and took the seat across from his brother.

"Mom says you have a girlfriend now. Is she pretty?" Jake eyed him curiously.

Collin laughed, "I have a friend who's a girl, and yes, she is very pretty."

Jake shot a quick look in Katrina's direction. He leaned forward to whisper in his brother's direction. "Remember that girl I told you about? The one with the cookies?"

Collin leaned across the table, meeting him halfway. He stole his own glance toward Katrina, who stood with her back to the two of them. "The pretty one with the long blond hair?"

Jake nodded. "I kissed her," he said, an air of pride pushing his chest forward.

Matthew chuckled, lifting his magazine a little higher to conceal the amusement painting his expression.

Collin grinned. "Cool, dude! I kissed my girl, too!" he said as he winked at the boy.

Jake sat back in his chair, his mile-wide smile filling his face.

Katrina suddenly dropped a plate of food in front of her eldest son as she turned her attention to the youngest. "Jacoby, you need to get moving. Mrs. Cyrus will be here any minute now to pick you up."

Jake frowned. "I thought you were driving today."

"I have to be in court early this morning, so Mrs. Cyrus and I traded days."

The youngster shook his head. "I hate when Mrs. Cyrus drives. She's always asking a lot of questions about Dad."

Katrina blinked. "What kind of questions?"

"Nosy questions!"

Matthew laughed.

Before Katrina could respond, a car horn sounded out in front of the home. Jake jumped from his seat, gulped the last of his orange juice, grabbed his backpack and rushed toward the door. Katrina hurried after him, admonishing the boy to not forget he had piano lessons after school and to remember to bring home his science book to work on his class project. Jake screamed his goodbyes from the front porch and then the house suddenly went quiet.

Matthew took another sip of his coffee, shifting his gaze toward Collin. "It's good to see you. We were starting to worry that you couldn't find your way home."

Collin felt his cheeks heat with color. He stammered, "I… W-we… It…"

His father held up his hand. "You don't need to explain it to me. Your mother might have some questions, though."

"His mother has nothing to say," Katrina suddenly interjected as she moved back into the room. She rounded the table, kissing one and then the other. "You're an adult and I'm just going to have to trust that we raised you to make responsible decisions. I will, however, ask that you make a concerted effort to spend some time with Jake. He idolizes you and I need you to be a role model he can depend on. And, when he's whispering to you about kissing some fast-tail little girl, that you remind him to always be respectful and careful, please. Don't high-five his antics!" She scoffed. "Like the two of you kissing girls is something to celebrate."

Collin laughed, "It is, actually. I didn't kiss a girl until I was in high school!"

Matthew laughed with his son.

Katrina rolled her eyes skyward. "Way too much information," she quipped. "I need to run. Do you think you can fit your old mom into your busy schedule? Maybe we can do lunch this week? Just the two of us?"

Collin nodded. "Just say when."

"Depending on the cases I get through today, maybe we can try for tomorrow."

"Just text me when you're sure. I'll make it work."

Katrina pressed her lips to her husband's. "Have a good day, baby!"

"I love you," Matthew responded. He tapped her backside as she turned, and she giggled as she rushed out the door.

"What time are you making?" Collin asked, reaching for his own cup of coffee.

"I have to head out in a few minutes, too," Matthew answered.

"Do you have some time for me to pick your brain?"

Matthew dropped his magazine to the table. "What's on your mind, son?"

"I think I'm falling in love with London, but she doesn't want a relationship."

"But she's sleeping with you?"

Collin felt himself blush a second time. "Something like that. How did you know with Mom? How were you certain you were in love?"

Matthew pondered the question briefly before he answered. "It was how I felt when we were apart," he finally said. "I couldn't breathe when your mother was away from me. I felt empty. When we were with each other, everything seemed possible. One day I realized I didn't want to be away from her. I couldn't imagine my life without her."

Collin sat in reflection, finishing the last of his pancakes.

"Why doesn't she want to be in a relationship?" Matthew asked.

Collin lifted his gaze back to his father's. He shook his head. "I'm not sure. Something happened in her past and I think she's scared."

Matthew nodded his head slowly. "If you two aren't on the same page, this could end badly. I wouldn't want to see you hurt. You need to think long and hard about continuing on the path you're on. If it's just sex for her, you need to be honest about that. And I won't tell you it's wrong, or that you shouldn't. I can only tell you to be smart. But it sounds like you and Ms. Jacobs still have to work on communicating with each other."

Collin blew a heavy gust of air past his full lips. He hadn't been able to stop thinking about London. He did miss her and despite what he'd said, he wanted more for the two of them than he'd actually admitted.

His father seemed to read his mind. "Talk to her, son. You need to be honest about your feelings, and she needs to be honest about hers. And just take your time. Neither one of you needs to rush. You're both still very young. God willing, you still have a whole lifetime ahead of you. If it's supposed to be, it will be."

The front desk receptionist at the Pro Bono Partnership greeted Collin warmly. "Good morning, Mr. Stallion!"

"Good morning, Ms. Bayer. How are you doing this morning?"

"Fine, thank you." The young woman tossed the length of her brunette hair over her shoulder as she batted her lashes. "You had a delivery, sir. I left the package on your desk."

Collin smiled his appreciation. "Thank you." He moved in the direction of his office. As he sauntered past London's office, she and her two friends were staring at him. He waved a hand and winked as he passed, disappearing into the office at the other end of the hall.

Felicia giggled as she turned back around in her seat. She and Paula exchanged a look with London. "So, have you had another date yet?" Felicia asked.

London shook her head. "No," she lied, shifting the

manila folders on her desk from one side to the other. "I told you it wasn't going anywhere."

Paula sighed. "We have such high hopes for you two."

London laughed, "I don't know why you two are so concerned about my love life."

"We want you to be happy," Paula stated.

London's smile lifted warmly. "I am very happy."

Perry suddenly peeked in, clearing his throat. Paula and Felicia both rose reluctantly.

"Good morning," the dynamic duo chimed simultaneously.

Perry nodded as he responded, "Good morning. Everyone have something to do this morning?"

"We're all good," London answered. "We were just discussing Mr. James."

Perry looked from Paula to Felicia and back. "Ms. Graves, Ms. Tyson, you two are the social workers assigned to Mr. James's case, correct?"

"That's correct," Paula answered. "I'll be visiting his family later this week to determine how we're going to be able to serve him best should he be released. Attorney Jacobs was just updating us on the current family dynamics."

"We just want to ensure we have a plan in place for housing, his financial needs, health care…" Felicia interjected, her voice trailing as she ticked off the rest of the list in her head.

Perry nodded again. "Carry on, then," he said as he resumed his stroll through the office.

Felicia laughed, "That man is so uptight! It's a wonder he doesn't explode."

The other two women laughed with her. Paula and Felicia headed to the door.

"Lunch later?" Paula queried.

"I'll let you know," London answered.

Before either could respond, Collin suddenly moved from his office to hers. "Sorry to interrupt," he said as he greeted each woman with a nod.

London waved a dismissive hand at her friends. "It's no problem. What's up?"

Collin passed her the oversize envelope he was carrying in his hands. "I think you should look at this," he said. He moved into the space, dropping into the seat that was just vacated. He sat watching her as London flipped through the documents inside.

Her eyes widened. "Are you absolutely sure about this?"

"It's what they sent from the prosecutor's office. We have no reason to doubt its validity."

"You know what this means, right?"

Collin nodded. "Yeah, Mr. James was railroaded. He should have never been charged with his wife's murder."

London swiped a tear from her eyes. "We need to file a motion for immediate dismissal of the charges."

"Already on it." Collin nodded. "I've also started a brief on Mr. James's behalf, detailing the prosecutorial misconduct. I want to include it with the motion to dismiss."

"You want to go after the original prosecution team?"

"What they did was flagrantly wrong. I want to

see that wrong corrected. Perry has given it his full support."

London locked gazes with the man. "Good work!"

He smiled. "I couldn't have done it without you."

There was a buzz in the office at the discovery of evidence that had never been passed to Jerome James's defense team at the time of his trial. There was the witness statement of the man's young son, who had been present during the murder. Six years old at the time, Jerome Junior had described the crime scene and the murder in detail, specifically stating that his daddy had not been home when the crime occurred. That a bad man had hurt his mommy. The neighbors had reported a strange man parked on the street near the James home, and the same man had been seen walking out of the nearby wooded area behind the house around the time of the killing. Weeks later, Mrs. James's wedding band had been recovered in a Houston pawnshop some two hundred miles away. The shop owner had given a statement that he'd received the ring from a young white male in his late teens or early twenties. Finally, the prosecutors had not called the chief investigator on the case to the stand, sending a red flag that something was amiss. Their entire case had been circumstantial, the prosecution team arguing that Jerome James's past militant behavior and community activism had made him a violent personality capable of murder.

Collin led the way into the courthouse, London following on his heels. They hoped that once they got their paperwork filed they could persuade the new county clerk to get them on the court calendar as soon as possible.

The woman at the counter, whom Collin had met the week before, looked like a great horned owl, with her horn-rimmed glasses and unique hairstyle. She glanced from Collin to London, her deadpan expression not giving them much confidence. Her name was Vivian Pratt and she lacked the robust personality of her predecessors.

"Does Judge Mays have anything this week?" London questioned. "Anything?"

Ms. Pratt cut an eye in London's direction, then resumed scrolling through her computer screen. "You already have a trial date set for next month," she said.

Collin nodded. "Yes, we do, but we're hoping we can get before a judge sooner, so we won't need to go to trial. Anything you can do would be greatly appreciated."

He smiled, leaning across the counter as he gave her a look. The woman smiled back, her mouth bending slowly upward.

"Let me see what I can do. I'll get your paperwork filed and then give your office a call later this afternoon."

"That would be great," Collin responded, still smiling sweetly.

The woman stamped the seal on the multiple copies of paperwork, then handed him a receipt. "Would you like me to call you directly?" she asked, her fingers accidently brushing against his hand as she returned his copies to him.

Collin shook his head. "Calling the office will be fine. Thank you so much, Ms. Pratt."

"You have a good day, Attorney Stallion." The woman shot London a look. "You, too," she said less enthusiastically as she spun back around toward her paperwork.

As they stepped out into the hallway, London gave him a look. "Really?"

"She was flirting with me," he said, grinning foolishly. "I didn't do anything to encourage it."

"But you used it to your advantage."

"I used it to *our* advantage," he answered.

London was just about to argue the point when she heard her name being called from the other side of the front foyer. She turned abruptly, searching out the familiar tenor. Without realizing it, she eased herself into Collin's side. She began to shake, the color draining from her face.

Collin sensed her distress as he pressed a heavy palm against her lower back. He called her name softly, his voice a low whisper, "London? You okay?"

She shook her head, tears misting her eyes. "Please, don't leave me," she muttered under her breath.

The man idling toward them was eyeing her keenly. Collin recognized Victor Wells from the news and media coverage of his recent nomination and appointment to the Texas Supreme Court. Justice Wells stood as tall as Collin, with a lankier build. His movie-star looks had served him well over the years, and Collin had often heard people say that Wells resembled a younger Clint Eastwood.

"London! Isn't this a surprise!" Wells exclaimed. He moved as if he wanted to pull London into a tight embrace, but she took a step back as Collin stepped forward protectively. Justice Wells came to a stop, looking from one to the other.

London didn't say anything, eyeing him with reservation.

The man extended a hand toward Collin. "Victor Wells, it's a pleasure."

"Collin Stallion, sir. It's a pleasure to meet you, Justice Wells."

"You aren't by any chance related to the Stallion family of Stallion Enterprises, are you?"

"My father is Matthew Stallion."

The judge nodded. He swung his attention back to London, who was still standing like stone, her arms wrapped tightly around her torso.

Collin saw what looked like fear in her eyes, her body braced as if she were ready to sprint if necessary.

Justice Wells persisted. "I've missed you, London. I've been keeping up with your career. I hear you picked up an old case I prosecuted when I was with the district attorney's office. James something or other."

Collin's eyes narrowed. "It's Jerome James."

Victor cut his eye at Collin. "Yeah. Whatever." He turned back to London. "I hate to see you waste your time. It was a solid conviction."

"Or not," Collin interjected.

Victor bristled. "Excuse me but I wasn't talking to you, young man. What is your relationship to London, anyway?"

The question seemed to snap London from the trance she'd fallen into. "None of your damn business," she snapped between clenched teeth. "Stay away from me or I will file for a restraining order."

Victor laughed, "And say what? All I've done is

try to have a casual conversation with you. Even Mr. Stallion would have to testify to that." Something dark crossed the man's face. He took a step toward her. When he did, London bristled, a hand reaching out for Collin and grabbing the back of his jacket as if to hide behind him. Victor's gaze narrowed, and his voice dropped an octave. His tone was suddenly less friendly. "I've got my eye on you, London. Don't think I don't," he said.

Victor took a step back, gave them both a slight nod of his head and then turned on his leather shoes, disappearing in the opposite direction. When he was no longer in sight, London released the breath she'd been holding. She gasped, sucking in oxygen like someone had been holding her underwater. The tears finally rolled down her cheeks. She was still shaking, and Collin barely recognized her. He wrapped his arms around her and held her tightly.

"Let's go," he said. "I'm taking you home."

"I need to get back to the office."

"You need to take a break."

He led her out the building and to her car. He settled her into the passenger seat, closing the door after she'd secured her seat belt. As she sat there, she looked completely lost, and he realized his nerves were still tense. He wasn't sure what it was, but something was amiss. He walked around the front of the car to the driver's seat and slid inside.

As he pulled the vehicle out of the parking lot and into traffic, neither noticed that Victor Wells was standing beside his own car watching them.

Chapter 8

London completely shut down. She had nothing to say to him as he drove them to her home. When they arrived at her apartment, she crawled into her bed, pulling the covers up over her head. She heard Collin on the phone with Perry, saying that she'd become sick at lunch and wasn't able to return. He insinuated he planned to take her to urgent care and then see her safely home. Then he promised to keep the man posted. She listened with half an ear, saying nothing at all.

London offered him little to explain her reaction to seeing Victor Wells. But even without her saying it out loud, Collin instinctively knew Victor had been the man who'd hurt her. The relationship that had gone all kinds of wrong. The love that had built walls of steel around her heart. He knew, and he wasn't quite sure how he felt about it.

He sat down on her bed, reaching a hand out to stroke her shoulder. He felt her body tense beneath his touch. He was half expecting her to pull away, but when she didn't he kicked off his shoes and stretched out onto the bed beside her. He wrapped his arms around her and pulled her against him, cradling his body around hers. She was suddenly crying again, low sobs that pulled at his heartstrings. He allowed her the moment, holding her tightly until she cried herself to sleep.

London had no idea how long she'd slept. It was dark out, the only reflection of light coming from the other side of her home. She sat up abruptly, startled as someone rattled pots and pans in her kitchen. Her anxiety lifted when she heard Collin singing along with the stereo that played softly in the living room. She took a deep breath and then a second, settling into the nervousness that deflated like a punctured balloon losing air.

She reached over to the nightstand and turned on the light. A soft glow illuminated the room. She stood up slowly, regaining her balance. As she moved toward the bathroom she noticed Collin's clothes folded neatly over the upholstered chair. She paused, trailing her finger across the silk fabric of his suit jacket.

She owed Collin an explanation and she had no idea where to begin. Explaining herself had never been an issue because she'd been a master at hiding the dirty secret she knew would have people eyeing her differently. This was the first time she hadn't been able to hide the fear she felt when seeing Victor Wells.

She had idolized her former professor. She had also loved him, imagining her future revolving around his. When he'd reciprocated her feelings, she'd been on cloud nine. As graduation had neared and she'd firmly established the first steps toward her future, Victor had suddenly become possessive and dictatorial. What she'd taken for confidence shifted into arrogance and his conservative demeanor more authoritarian. His compliments were backhanded affronts that were more insulting than kind. Arguments became major battles, with him screaming obscenities at her. The first time he slapped her she hadn't known what to do. The infraction had shocked her, and then the apology had been lavish. Everything after became secret. Lies were abundant, as she turned the explanation of her bruises into an art form. He'd separated her from her friends and family and had ensured everything she said and did revolved around him.

For two years no one knew the abuse she endured. She was ashamed and embarrassed that her life had completely crashed and burned beneath the weight of his fists. The last beating had put her in the hospital with a broken jaw, fractured pelvis, blackened eyes and scars that would last her the rest of her life. Held hostage by the fear of what he promised to do if she ever told, she'd been unable to point a finger at him, refusing to name her assailant when asked. The day she'd been released she'd run home to her parents and had hidden herself away for months. Victor hadn't followed.

They'd only had one encounter after, when Vic-

tor had cornered her in a local grocery store and had
threatened that it would only be over when he said.
That time would never be her friend and she would
always belong to him. He had his eyes on her, he'd
professed, and he always would. He had leaned in
and kissed her cheek before disappearing as quickly
as he'd arrived. She had urinated on herself from fear.
One week later Victor had married, and remained
wedded to the woman until now. London had thought
herself free. She'd watched his career from afar. Had
managed to keep her distance, never running into him
in the courtroom. She'd changed her circle of friends
and had prayed daily that they never crossed paths
again. She became protective of her space, not allowing any man to get but so close. Until Collin. And
now Victor was back, and she was petrified. Her fear
was corporeal, so thick and putrid that she could feel
it sucking her down like quicksand.

London resumed her trek to the toilet. After empty-
ing her bladder, she washed her hands and face, then
headed out to the kitchen. Collin was standing at the
stove in nothing but his boxer briefs, socks and one
of her kitchen aprons. He was stirring something in a
pot, the decadent aroma that filled the room inciting
her hunger. He grinned as she moved into his space,
opening his arms widely as she stepped against him.
Her arms glided around his waist as she pressed her
cheek to his chest.

"Hey, sleepy!" he greeted as he kissed her forehead.
"You're finally awake."

"How long did I sleep?"

"It's been a good six hours," he said gesturing toward the large clock on the wall.

"You've been here the whole time?"

"Most of it. I ran back to the office and then to the supermarket," he said.

"What did you tell Perry?"

"That you just had a twenty-four-hour bug. That you would probably be doing better tomorrow."

"Thank you." She slid from him, moving to the counter and one of the high stools. In her head she wanted to express her appreciation that he wasn't asking questions she wasn't prepared to answer. Because she was grateful for the reprieve, able to pretend for a few minutes longer that everything was well.

Collin poured her a glass of red wine and refilled his own. "Are you hungry?"

"Famished!"

"Good. I made my famous spaghetti and meat sauce. I just need to toast the garlic bread and then we can eat."

"Where did you learn to cook?"

"My mother. She's an expert at quick and fast meals. This recipe has always been one of my favorites."

"It smells really good!"

Collin tipped a wooden spoon into the pot of red sauce. He cupped his palm beneath the spoon as he moved to where she sat. He lifted the spoon to her lips to give her a taste. London blew a breath to cool the heat before sipping at the sauce he offered.

She purred and then she smacked her lips. "This is good!" There was an air of surprise in her voice.

"You say that like you're surprised."

"I am!" she said with a soft giggle.

He swatted a kitchen towel in her direction. "Hater! I can't believe you doubted me!"

London laughed with him. Her emotions seemed to shift into normal and she felt like all was well again. Minutes later, Collin had the food plated, their wineglasses refilled, and both were eating heartily. The conversation was easy and comfortable, almost as if what had happened earlier had only been a bad dream. He didn't bring up the subject of Victor Wells and neither did she. London still wasn't sure she was ready to open herself to the scrutiny she knew would inevitably come.

When the meal was done and finished the two stood together to wash and dry the dishes. After her kitchen was clean and back to normal, Collin pulled a container of black cherry ice cream from the freezer and filled two bowls with the icy confection. Crispy sugar cookies and the soft lull of Anthony Hamilton completed dessert.

"What are you doing on Sunday?" London asked.

Collin dropped his bowl and spoon onto the coffee table. "I don't have anything planned. What do you have in mind?"

"I promised my mother I would go to church. I was hoping you'd come with me. I'd love for you to meet my parents."

His smile stretched full across his face. "The parents! That sounds pretty serious."

"It's not that serious," she said with a shake of her head. "Don't get it twisted!"

He chuckled, "No, I'm going to take it very seriously!"

London rolled her eyes skyward.

Collin continued, "I think I can make that happen.

Thank you. I'd love to join you. Now, what are you doing Saturday?"

"Saturday?"

"Yeah, you know, the day before Sunday?"

"It depends."

"Depends on what?"

"On what you have planned?"

"I'd like for you to come to the ranch and spend the day with me."

"At your family's ranch?"

"No, your family's ranch!" he said sarcastically. "What other ranch would I be talking about?" he laughed.

London narrowed her gaze on him, tossing him a look. Something in his tone had struck a nerve. For a split second she thought to respond with her own snarky comment, but she held her tongue. She couldn't, however, stall the look that crossed her face.

Concern suddenly washed over Collin's face. "I was just teasing, London," he said. "I didn't mean to offend you. Did I offend you?"

She turned to stare into his eyes. The emotion seeping from his eyes teased every one of her sensibilities. She pressed her palm to the side of his face.

"No, of course not. I know you were just trying to be funny. Your sense of humor stinks, though. It's a good thing you're an attorney and not a comedian." She lifted herself up to press a kiss against his lips. "I would love to spend the day at your family ranch on Saturday. Can I ride a horse?"

He smiled. "Of course. In fact, if you need some practice I have a horse right here that you can...well..."

He lifted his eyebrows suggestively, an amused smirk on his face.

London laughed, "I'm sure there's a stallion joke in there somewhere, too!"

Delight rang through the air as they laughed heartily. The sound system continued to play music, and two songs later, they sat quietly together. London couldn't help wondering if all their evenings with each other could be so peaceful. Being with Collin, had become her favorite thing in the world to do. She enjoyed every minute they were in each other's company and despite thinking she needed to talk herself out of a relationship with him, deep down inside she wanted him in her life more than she had wanted anything else in a very long time. If they could be like this for the rest of their lives, she thought, everything would be perfect. But despite her best efforts, there wasn't enough fantasy to sway the elephant that lingered like an unwanted guest in the room.

"He used to beat me," she suddenly said. "Victor Wells used to beat me. During our relationship he was physically and verbally abusive and he made my life a living hell."

Collin reached for his glass of wine. As he ruminated over the admission he suddenly realized he was holding his breath. He exhaled, sighing heavily. "I'm sorry you had to experience that," he finally said. "Do you want to talk about it?" He shifted forward in his seat, turning so they faced each other. He studied her intently. "You know you can tell me anything, right?"

For a moment, London didn't answer and then everything in her wanted him to know everything there was to know about her. She nodded and then she started at the beginning, telling the story no one else in her life knew. She detailed the brutality that had ravaged her self-esteem. She left no detail untold, questioning her own motives for staying when she should have run. For hiding when she should have exposed Victor for the monster that he was. When she was finished, tears misted Collin's eyes. Hers rained down over her cheeks, dampening the front of her blouse.

"You're still frightened of him, aren't you?" Collin questioned.

London nodded. "He scares the hell out of me. I thought I'd gotten past it, but…well…" She shrugged her narrow shoulders.

Collin reached for her hand and entwined his fingers with hers. "I won't let anything happen to you, London. Ever. He will never be able to hurt you like that again."

She shook her head. She desperately wanted to believe him, but she didn't. Collin didn't know the monster she knew. The man who, in the beginning of her career, had cost her job after job just by implying she had emotional issues. Interjecting himself when she least expected. He had leveraged his professional position against her as easily as he'd given her glowing recommendations when it suited him. Collin couldn't begin to know the cruelty, the threats or the pain that Victor had inflicted against her. The hours she'd cowered in the corner of his home, too petrified to even take herself to the bathroom. The days she'd spent locked in the dank basement, cut off from everything and everyone she loved. Having to sometimes beg him for a drink of water and needing his permission to simply speak. No one knew that man and she hadn't trusted anyone would have believed her if she told.

Every year since there was some reminder—an unsigned Christmas card, an anonymous drink sent to her table, telephone calls that were wrong numbers, something that kept her on edge and reminded her he was still too close for her to relax and feel safe. There were brief periods when there was nothing: the man seeming to have moved on and then just like that, she would know beyond any doubt, that he was back, keeping an eye on her like he'd promised.

She couldn't begin to explain to anyone how bad it had gotten. Or hope they could understand that no matter how it seemed as if she'd been able to go on with her life and he with his, she was terrified he would one day make good on his threats to steal her joy and end her life, when he was good and ready to be done with her.

Sensing the magnitude of emotion that consumed her, Collin wrapped his arms around her shoulders and pulled her toward him. For a split second she flinched and then she didn't, allowing herself to relax into his arms.

The mood had them both in their feelings. Needing to lighten the moment, Collin changed the subject. "So," he said, "are we still just best friends?"

London laughed, "Maybe!"

"Maybe?"

"You're still getting benefits, aren't you?"

"I hope so. You haven't cut me off already, have you?"

She smiled, lifting her gaze to his. "I'll tell you

what, how about we graduate you to boyfriend? Is that better?"

Collin grinned. "For now!"

Collin had lost track of time. He and London had spent hours talking and then she'd finally fallen asleep. She snored softly beside him, but he couldn't rest, lost in a state of wakefulness that felt never ending. It pained him immensely to know that someone had raised their hands against London. He couldn't begin to fathom the coward who would do such a thing.

He'd seen more than his fair share of domestic violence cases litigated. He had witnessed victims testifying in court about horrific abuses. He'd also seen the families of victims who hadn't survived. At the ranch he'd spent time with kids who'd lost a parent or had their lives turned upside down, their families destroyed, when one parent savagely attacked the other. Each and every time that he tried to understand the mind-set of a man who could hurt the person he professed to love, he couldn't. He just couldn't. There weren't enough excuses in the world for anyone to justify violence against another individual.

Now all he could think of was how to protect London. Because London had become his whole entire world and he would do whatever he needed to do to ensure her safety. As he contemplated going up against the likes of the Honorable Justice Wells, Collin knew the challenge he and London might face wouldn't be easy. But they had each other, and their families, and he knew, beyond any doubt, that she had a greater chance of beating her demon with him there to fight with her, than by her lonesome.

London muttered something in her sleep as she rolled closer to him, seeking out his body heat. He stared down at her, in awe of how beautiful she was. She looked peaceful, finally resting comfortably. She slept on her back, one leg curled with her manicured foot against her calf. Her bottom lip trembled, and he suspected she was dreaming, her eyes twitching rapidly behind her closed lids.

He had often wondered what his parents had felt for each other as they'd fallen head over heels in love. He remembered the dates and romantic trips his father had lavished on his mother, anxious for her attention. He remembered how giddy she'd been, excited at the mere mention of his father's name. For the first time, it clicked, making sense in a way he hadn't known possible. Because what he was feeling for London felt monumental. It had taken on a life of its own and was growing with an intensity that had him speechless. It filled him abundantly and he found himself unable to imagine his life without her. Picturing such a thing made his heart hurt; it felt as if the organ itself had been pierced with a blade.

She rolled again, curling her backside against him as she pulled her body into the fetal position. With a deep breath Collin turned and curved himself around her. He reached for the covers, pulling the sheets and blanket up and tucking them around both their bodies. Her eyes fluttered open for the briefest moment, and she reached for his hand, pulling his arm around her waist. She smiled sweetly, a soft snore blowing past her parted lips. Collin nuzzled his face into the back of her neck, inhaling the scent of her perfume that lingered against her skin. He whispered a prayer of thanksgiving, breathing in and out slowly as he finally drifted off to sleep.

Chapter 9

The rest of their workweek ended without mishap. Collin and London came to work and left, doing their jobs. Neither brought up the subject of Justice Wells again, despite thoughts of the man lingering in the back of both their minds.

Vivian Pratt at the clerk's office had come through for them, and they had a court date scheduled for the following Tuesday. They reviewed every ounce of evidence for the umpteenth time. When they were certain, beyond any reasonable doubt, that their case was solid, they paid Mr. James a visit to prepare him for what would come.

When the man entered the visitors' room, his demeanor was as nonchalant as it had been that first time Collin had met him. He eyed them both warily, nothing about their presence striking a chord with him.

"Mr. James! How are you, sir?" Collin said, his casual tone meant to put the man at ease.

"Stallion, right?"

"Yes, sir."

Mr. James's gaze swept from Collin to London. "So, what's good, Ms. Jacobs?"

London got directly to the point. "The judge will hear our petition for dismissal of all charges against you on Tuesday. They'll bring you down to the courthouse at nine o'clock. Your son will bring a suit for you to change into. I'll present all the evidence and argue for your acquittal. By the grace of God, you'll be a free man by lunchtime."

Mr. James nodded his head slowly. A slight smile lifted his lips. "My son came to see me. He's able to come regularly since I'm here. Hopefully, if things don't work out, they'll transfer me to someplace close. I'm getting old, so if there is anything you can do to make that happen I'd appreciate it."

Collin gave the man a slight smile. "Mr. James, we're going to do everything we can to send you home with your son next week. That's our goal and we're not going to let you down, sir. I know it's hard for you to trust that, but we will do whatever it takes to vindicate you and get you back to your life."

Mr. James appraised him, seemingly trying to decide if he could trust what Collin was promising. He sat forward in his seat, his hands clasped tightly together atop the table. "You might not understand this, son, but it's hard to have any hope. Hope died the day my wife was murdered. Now I take each day one at a time and deal with whatever may come." He shifted back in the wooden chair. "Do you have someone special in your life, son?"

Collin nodded. "Yes, sir. I do." He shot a quick look in London's direction.

"Are you in love?"

Collin inhaled swiftly, the question catching him off guard. "Yes, sir," he finally answered, "I think I am." He was still staring directly at the old man, hesitant to look in London's direction a second time.

London's head snapped as she turned to stare at him. His answer surprised her, a wealth of emotion exploding across her face. When he finally did cast his eyes on her he gave her the warmest smile and a slight nod of his head.

Mr. James sat pensively, still staring at Collin. "It's a precious thing, love. Hold tight to it. You never know how long it's going to last or when it will leave you. I don't imagine I'll ever know love like that again in my lifetime."

London hadn't known what to expect when she pulled through the gates of Stallion-Briscoe Ranch. What she hadn't expected was the long list of activities that Collin had prepared for them. As she pulled her car into an empty parking spot he stood on the front porch of the massive family home, waving excitedly.

She heard herself hum with appreciation. Collin looked great and she was suddenly breathing heavy with wanting. Tight Levi's jeans fitted the high shelf of his very round behind, the length of black denim covering his black cowboy boots. A bright white cotton shirt was buttoned midway up his broad chest, exposing just a hint of caramel skin, and a classic black

Stetson hat sat perched on top of his head. He epito-
mized her cowboy fantasy, the horse the only thing
missing from the fairy tale.

She could barely contain her own excitement as she
crossed the stone driveway and met him at the bottom of the steps. "Good morning!" she exclaimed as
she threw her arms around his neck and kissed him.

"Good morning. How are you doing?" he asked as
he wrapped her in a bear hug.

"Nervous! And I'm not sure why."

"Don't be nervous. I just want you to relax and
have a good day."

Light shimmered in her eyes as she met his stare.
She pushed her hands into the pockets of her denim
jeans, the gesture emphasizing the tight fit around
her slight curves. "So, what's on the agenda today?"

"I thought we'd play it by ear. My mom's inside
and the aunts are making breakfast."

"Breakfast?"

"It's not like the family gatherings we have on Sundays, but it'll be a good meal. Biscuits, gravy, sausage,
bacon, eggs, grits, toast. Maybe even some pancakes
if we get lucky. Usually, on Sundays, everyone shows
up for breakfast and there's a feast, but there'll only
be a few of us today."

London's eyes widened, a hint of anxiety seeping
from her stare.

"They're all going to love you," he said, reading
her mind.

London didn't bother to respond as he grabbed her
hand and pulled her along and into the family home.

"The Stallion Foundation is hosting an event at
the conference center this afternoon. I thought we

could volunteer for a little bit. Maybe go down and help pass out gift bags or something. Afterward we'll head to the stables, saddle up the horses and I'll take you exploring."

London shot him a look and a nod. "That sounds like it's going to be a long day!"

"I just want you to relax and have a good time."

She stopped short at the door. "Thank you," she said as Collin eyed her curiously. "You make me smile and I feel pretty darn special when I'm with you."

He kissed her mouth. "It's what boyfriends do!"

They were giggling like grade-schoolers when they entered the home's oversize family room. Katrina, Michelle and Marah were talking politics with John and Matthew when they entered the room. The conversation came to an abrupt halt, everyone turning to stare.

London tossed up an anxious hand in greeting. "Good morning," she chimed, a hint of nervousness in her voice.

"Good morning, London," Katrina said as she rose from her seat. "Welcome to the ranch!" She gave the young woman a warm hug and then reached to kiss her son.

"Thank you for having me, Judge Stallion."

"Hey, all, this is my *girlfriend*, London Jacobs," Collin interjected as he introduced her to his family, everyone greeting her warmly. The emphasis he put on the word *girlfriend* didn't go unnoticed.

"London, would you like some coffee?" Marah asked.

"Thank you! That would be great!"

"Help yourself to food," Michelle added. "There is plenty!"

"Do you want pancakes?" Collin asked as he grabbed two plates from the counter and began to fill one with bacon.

She shook her head as she dropped into a chair. "Just some fruit, please, and maybe a slice of toast."

"The women in this family have hearty appetites," John chimed. "So don't be shy!"

"I know that's right!" Mitch exclaimed as she reached for a second biscuit and slathered it with butter and honey.

"So, London, where are you from?" Marah asked.

"Dallas, born and raised," she answered.

"And you're an attorney, too, is that right?" John questioned.

London nodded. "Yes, sir."

Collin dropped down into the seat beside London, passing her a plate of fruit salad, toast and a few slices of bacon. For the next half hour they peppered her with questions. In no time at all she was bantering back and forth with the lot of them, her comfort levels having risen exponentially. She joined in as they resumed their discussion on the political climate and weighed in her opinion when Katrina announced that she was considering an election run for a senate seat.

"You'd be a great candidate, Judge Stallion! I would love to support your campaign."

"I appreciate that, London, but I'm still undecided."

"You've done so much for young women in the community. We need someone with your values representing us. You'd be an excellent voice for the constituents of Texas, and with your record, we could trust that you would always put people before party."

Collin nodded his agreement. "We definitely

wouldn't have to worry about you facing the same ethical dilemmas our current senate representatives have to contend with. You'd never take donations from anyone lobbying for their own interests. I think it's a fantastic idea, Mom!"

Matthew gave his wife a look. "I wholeheartedly agree, and I told you we would all support you if you decide to do it."

"I'll make a decision in the next day or two. I just need to think about it for a bit longer."

"Please, let me know how I can help," London added. "I stuff a mean envelope!"

Katrina smiled and nodded.

Mark Stallion suddenly rushed into the room. "Great! You're all here. We're going to need some serious help this afternoon. We have some thirty-two families from the shelter here for Family Fun Day. The crowd is already lining up," he said as he poured himself a cup of coffee. His gaze swept around the room, pausing as his eyes met London's. His brow rose in curiosity.

"Hey, Uncle Mark, this is London. My girlfriend!" Collin said, a cheesy grin spreading across his face.

Mark moved to London's side, looking from her to Collin and back. He extended his hand to shake hers. "It's very nice to meet you, London. I'm Collin's favorite uncle, Mark Stallion."

"The pleasure is mine, sir. Your nephew speaks of you often."

Mark grinned. "Nephew!" he exclaimed loudly. He moved to his own seat, giving Collin a look and pointing his index finger at the young man. He nodded enthusiastically. "You go, boy!" he said as he gave him two thumbs pointed toward the ceiling.

The men in the room all burst out laughing. London felt herself blush, color heating her cheeks.

Michele rolled her eyes skyward. "Don't pay them any mind, London. Not one of them has an ounce of good sense."

London giggled, "It's fine. I appreciate the compliment."

Collin leaned into her, kissing her cheek, and she felt herself blush even more.

When the meal was finished, they headed down to the conference center as Collin gave her a condensed tour of the massive estate. They took a shortcut through the rose gardens behind the main homestead and she inhaled the sweet aroma of the lush foliage.

"This is beautiful!" London gushed as she took in the edged flower beds, bricked paths, trellised archways and the exquisite fountain that the entire garden design fed from. The roses themselves were blooming abundantly, a profusion of rich coloration painting the landscape.

Collin held her hand as he guided her along the paths. "I never really appreciated the space when I was a kid. It was just a bunch of plants and flowers, but now I like to sit out here when I need to think things through. It's quite relaxing."

"No doubt," London said as she imagined herself returning to the space to just sit and take things in. "I would just love to sit here and read."

"When I had to fulfill my community service requirements and we started coming here, that's what my mom would do while she waited for me. She and my aunt Marah both say it's their refuge away from the daily grind of just being women in high demand."

"I can see that. I hope I have an opportunity to just come sit one day."

He squeezed her fingers. "Whenever you want," he said.

Exiting the gardens, Collin led her down a path to a golf cart. They climbed aboard and traveled some distance from the home to the other side of the massive estate. The large brick community center bore the Briscoe family emblem and name and Collin told her about Edward, the patriarch who'd once been a cowboy with a dream.

"He sounds like a riot," she said, laughing.

"His age has finally caught up with him and his health is failing but occasionally I can get him out to ride around on the golf cart with me."

"I hope I can meet him one day," she said.

"You will. There's still plenty more family for you to meet. I'm just hoping they don't scare you off!"

Inside, the rest of Collin's family had already begun to direct the activities. Men, women and children from local homeless shelters had been invited to come for lunch. There were activities for the kids, social workers present to help parents who needed guidance with job searches and rental applications, financial advisors offering banking and credit advice, and doctors and nurses to treat minor health issues and ensure inoculations and flu shots were up to date. A team of Stallion employees handed out meals and assisted wherever they were needed.

Collin and London jumped right in. They directed games and played with toddlers. Both donned plastic caps and gloves to spoon up barbecue and potato salad onto paper plates. They passed out bags of canned goods, hygiene products and coupons for discounted services and literature about available services in the community. Together and separately they moved about the space, talking to and laughing with people. Everyone seemed to be having a great time.

At one point, Collin found himself staring at her. London sat across the room in conversation with two elderly women. She was animated, her face gleaming with joy, and the two women were laughing with her. When she rose from her seat, she hugged them both, pressing her cheek to theirs. Everything about her made his heart sing. She was enjoying herself and looked completely at ease.

His uncle Mark interrupted his musings. "London is quite charming."

Collin cast a glance toward the man, who had moved to his side. "She's something special, Uncle Mark."

"I can tell. Your parents speak quite highly of her, as well. Even your mother, and we didn't think she'd ever like anyone you were dating. It helps when your people like your girl."

Collin nodded. "I love her. I haven't told her. Not directly, but I think she knows. I really do love her."

Mark slapped him against the back. "I can see it all over your face."

"Is it that obvious?"

"To those of us who know you. Have you met her people yet?"

"Not yet. But I'm going to church with her and her parents tomorrow."

"Her father is going to want to know your intentions. Just be honest. If you're not sure, it's okay to say that. He'll respect you for it."

"What if he doesn't like me?"

Mark laughed, "Look at you all nervous!"

"I… W-well…" Collin suddenly stammered.

"It'll be fine. Just be yourself and you won't have anything to worry about." Mark slapped him on his back a second time. "I appreciate you two coming out to help. We're about to wrap things up, so if you want to sneak off you can."

"Thanks. I thought I'd take her riding and show her around the property."

"Make sure you take her down to the pond. After the rose garden, Stallion women love that damn pond!"

Collin had often talked about the stables and horses on Stallion ranch. London didn't really comprehend what it all meant to him until they were there, and she saw him thriving in the midst of it. There was something that came over him as he stroked the muzzle of the horse he had named Baby. Something that made her feel immensely blessed to witness it as he murmured softly to the large animal.

"How often do you have to clean the stables?" she asked.

"Daily. If you don't, it makes for a longer, harder, smellier job later. It's also harder on the back," Collin advised, adding that it was wise to strip the stall down to the bare floor once a week and let it air-dry for the day before adding new bedding. "My mornings usually start here when I'm home."

London listened intently as he detailed all that needed to be done and how best to do it. She couldn't begin to imagine herself following his lead and attempting to muck the stalls. Just the thought of the pungent aroma of horse burning in her nostrils gave her pause. She made a face and Collin laughed.

"It's really not that bad," he said. "You get used to it. You just need to make sure you aim into the wheelbarrow!" He kicked at the fresh hay that had been laid out for the animals.

He led her back outside, standing at the edge of one of four paddocks. London admired the horses that grazed lazily about. There were five before them, four chestnut brown in color. One black horse rounded out the group.

"How many horses do you have?" she asked, genuine interest in her voice.

"We can board up to eighty at a time. Thirty of them are ours, though. We now have twenty stallions that we use for breeding and the others we use for teaching. My aunt Marah and her sisters have their horses here. My dad and I also have our own horses."

"Since I don't know a lot about horses, tell me what makes a stallion different from all the other horses." She leaned with her back against the fence, turning to face him.

"The stallion is a male horse that has not been castrated. They usually have a thicker neck compared to a mare or a gelding. They also have very muscular physiques and are known for their fiery temperaments."

London smiled as he continued.

"Stallions can also be more unpredictable than other horses. But that fire can give them a competitive edge. Typically, they can exhibit sex-driven dominance behaviors and they might bite, or square up and rear. Only experienced handlers should ride a stallion."

London chuckled softly, "Stallions owning stallions. That's quite novel!"

Collin laughed. He reached a large hand out to brush a stray hair from her forehead.

London found herself leaning into his touch, and so she took a step toward him, easing her arms around his waist. "You are quite the wealth of information! Your barnyard knowledge is very impressive."

"Barnyard knowledge! Now, that's cute!"

"Not as cute as you are," she said as she nuzzled her face into the curve of his neck, inhaling the scent of his cologne. She kissed the soft flesh, then licked the salt from his skin. "So, do I get to ride?"

"Have you ridden before?"

London shook her head. "Not since I was seventeen, maybe eighteen."

"Then I'll give you a choice. I can saddle you your own horse for you to ride or you can ride one with me."

"That wouldn't hurt the horse?"

"We have a sturdy draft horse who would be fine. We won't go at a full gallop, maybe just canter. And we won't go too far for too long."

London nodded. "Then tandem it is!"

Collin led the horse named Trapper out of his stall. The animal was impressive, heavy on muscle and nicely bulked. His legs were long and solid. Collin moved to Trapper's left shoulder and tossed a blanket onto his back. He opted to forgo the saddle so that they could be more comfortable. He bridled the horse and checked the bit placement, the curb strap, throatlatch and the earpiece. After ensuring everything was in place, he decided they were ready to ride.

He threw his leg up and over the horse's back, mounting him easily. When Trapper brayed his approval, he reached his hand out to London. With strength that surprised her, he pulled her up so that she could mount the horse's back behind him. She wrapped her arms around his torso, clasping her hands together over his chest. When Collin was certain that she was comfortable, he nudged the horse with his knees and they took off.

They meandered slowly across the pristine fields to allow the horse to adjust to their weight. London pressed herself against his back, allowing herself to settle comfortably against him. As they both relaxed, the horse relaxed with them, the trio moving easily as if they were one singular unit.

The air was heated, the afternoon sun sitting bright and full in a deep blue sky. London filled her lungs, then blew a heavy gust slowly past her lips. It was a beautiful afternoon to ride. They headed toward the edge of the estate, disappearing into the line of trees that skirted the property. As Collin guided them deeper and deeper into the brush, London enjoyed the ride, savoring the beauty of their excursion.

Minutes later the trees parted, and they found themselves in a clearing whose beauty took London's breath away. The grassy knoll was a plethora of blooming flowers that surrounded a small pond with a cascading waterfall. It was nirvana. Excitement bubbled like a fresh spring in her midsection.

"This is beautiful!" she cooed as Collin helped her to dismount. She pressed her palm to his chest. "Absolutely beautiful!"

Collin lifted the blanket from Trapper's back. The horse began to graze, finding his own peace in the afternoon heat. He reached for London's hand and guided her to the water's edge. As London stood staring out over the landscape, Collin spread the blanket across the ground. He moved to her side and wrapped his arms around her torso as she leaned back against him, taking in the magnificent view. He nuzzled his face into her hair, inhaling the sweet scent of coconut oil and hibiscus along the strands.

They stood together for some time, both enamored with the view, and each other. The moment was surreal.

"I'm going to say something," London started, "and if anyone ever asks me about it, I will deny it."

Collin gave her a look, glancing down at her. "What?"

"I kind of like this boyfriend-girlfriend thing. In fact, I think I like it a lot."

"Is that right?"

"Yes."

"Then I'm making some serious progress." Collin grinned.

"You good with that?"

"For now," he said with a hearty laugh.

London spun around in his arms to face him, clutching the front of his shirt as she leaned up to press a kiss to his mouth. He tasted sweet, like the sugared candy he'd been sucking on all afternoon. When he parted her lips with his tongue, easing into her mouth, the sensation wafted through her like an explosive device that had been detonated with full force. The kiss was passionate and possessive, Collin claiming her with his lips. She pressed her body tightly to his, aware that he had hardened in his jeans, an erection pressing urgently between them. The deluge of emotion had rocked them both.

London pulled herself from him. "Have you brought all of your girlfriends here?"

His mouth lifted in a sly smile. "I haven't brought any girls here. You are the first, and something tells me that you will be the last."

London grinned. "So, what are the chances someone might walk up on us?"

Collin shook his head. "Highly unlikely. What do you have in mind?"

The smile on London's face was teasing as she took a step back. She began to unbutton her shirt, slowly releasing the fasteners one by one. Collin watched her as she pushed the garment off one shoulder and then the other. He eyed her hungrily as she exposed a black lace bra and inch after inch of warm brown skin. She dropped the garment to the ground and then stepped out of her jeans. She stood naked before him, wearing nothing but a pair of boy shorts in black, and then those were lying on the ground, as well.

Collin cupped his palm over his crotch, his male member feeling as if it were ready to implode with pleasure. The look in his eye was one of pure hunger. Had there been a roof above their heads his pulse and heart rate would have blown a hole through it. There was a knot in his throat and suddenly his mouth was dry as he broke out into a sweat.

The beautiful woman stepped into him, her body so close to his that he could hear her breathing, each inhalation and exhalation fluttering through her lungs. Sliding one hand behind his neck, she pulled him down to her and kissed him again, capturing his lips with reckless abandon. She shivered uncontrollably when Collin dropped both hands to her hips, gliding her body against his own.

London pulled at his clothes, unbuttoning his shirt and his pants, pulling frantically until he was free from his clothes. She kissed him again, gently at first, and then she opened her mouth to him, her tongue dancing excitedly with his. Collin clutched the back of her neck and deepened the kiss even more.

Easing her down to the blanket, Collin kissed her neck, nibbling gently at her flesh. London moaned her pleasure into the late-afternoon air, the sound of it blowing in the warm breeze. She savored the sensation of his touch as he glided his hands up and down the length of her body.

They rolled from one side to the other and back again until London was lying on top of him. Collin reclaimed her lips, one hand tangled in her hair, the other clutching the round of her butt cheeks. Both moaned at the skin-on-skin contact. Easing his hand between her legs he pushed his fingers into her, administering to the bundle of swollen flesh that pulsed beneath his fingers. It was almost too much to bear as London fell into a trance of sheer pleasure. She gyrated her hips, grinding her pelvis against his hand as she moaned his name over and over again.

Collin sat upright and flipped her onto her back. He reached for his jeans and a condom hidden in his pants pocket. He sheathed himself quickly, then slid his body into hers, dipping into the puddle of wetness that had pooled between her thighs. His strokes were long and slow as he caressed her inner lining with the length of himself. They loved each other as if it were the first time, the magnificence of it sweeping waves of pleasure through them. Collin captured her mouth one more time, his mouth dancing against hers as he savored the taste of her.

He could feel her orgasm building, every nerve ending sliding toward the edge as her body began to convulse around his. His own orgasm suddenly ripped through him. She screamed his name, the lilt of it echoing through the air. Tears of joy washed past her lashes, her words melting into an incoherent jumble. Collin's own spasms rippled through every muscle in his body. They were both swept away, everything feeling bigger and brighter. Sensation swept through the open air, the coloration of the flora and the sound of the waterfall vibrating through every fiber of their beings.

When Collin collapsed above her, they were both spent with exhaustion. They lay side by side for some time, trading gentle caresses and light kisses as the sun began to settle low in the brilliant blue sky.

Collin lifted herself up on an elbow to look down at her. "I love you, London," he said softly. "I know you heard me when I said it to Mr. James the other day. I also know why you didn't mention it and we never discussed it. But I do, London. I've fallen head over heels in love with you."

London felt her heart begin to race. Because she hadn't been ready to talk about his feelings. Or her own. And even in that moment the thoughts suddenly racing through her head petrified her. The joy hanging onto the tailwind of her feel-good was playing hide-and-seek with a whole host of emotions.

Collin seemed to understand. He leaned down to kiss her one more time. "I love you. And when you're ready to say it back, I will be right here."

She lifted her eyes to his. "And you're good with that?" she whispered, expectation lingering in her tone.

"For now," he whispered back and then he kissed her one more time.

Chapter 10

London's good mood had lasted through the night and well into the morning. The early alarm she'd set pulled them both from a night of sweet dreams. They'd made love before rising to shower, dress and head to her family's church. Even now she could still feel the warmth of him covering her body. His touch still burned hot, the pressure of his hands feeling as though they'd never left her skin and London was amazed that she was still so acutely aware of him even though they sat in different rooms of the modest family home.

Collin and her father were enjoying an old movie, laughing hysterically at the 1995 film *Friday* with Ice Cube and Chris Tucker. Despite her own intense dislike for the movie, she was thoroughly amused by how amused the two of them were. To her surprise, the two men had taken to each other, coming together like long-lost friends who were reunited. Collin had hit it off famously with everyone, the old women of the church smitten by his good looks and dazzling smile. He'd charmed the entire congregation, including her parents, and now it was as if he'd always been one of the family.

London sat at the kitchen table, watching her mother as she puttered between the counters and the stove. The aroma of fried chicken wafted through the air and the matriarch was putting the final finishes on a broccoli salad while she waited for an oversize pan of macaroni and cheese to be finished in the oven. London rose from her seat to peek in on the men. Both were laughing, completely enthralled by some joke that she knew she wouldn't find funny. She turned back to her mother.

"Are you sure there isn't anything I can do to help?"

"No, dear. The table is set and as soon as the macaroni's done we'll be able to eat. Just sit back, relax and talk to me. Tell me about you and your young man. How long have you two been dating?"

"It hasn't been that long. He started working with the firm a month or two ago and we've been seeing each other for just a few weeks."

Her mother grinned. "Your daddy and I only dated for a month before we got married. We knew we were in love the first time we saw each other."

"Daddy says he wasn't sure until you told him."

He mother laughed, "And he's been the happiest man in the world since," she said matter-of-factly.

London smiled. Her parents' love story had always fascinated her. How her prim and proper mother had fallen so quickly for the aspiring musician who'd become a high school music teacher. Friends and family had placed bets on how long the couple would last, losing with each anniversary they celebrated. Since that fateful Saturday afternoon, they'd celebrated forty-five years of marital bliss.

There'd been a time London had imagined that for herself. A love so fanciful that it would have been fodder for a romantic fairy tale. For a brief period, she thought she'd found that with Victor, and then just like that their relationship had gone dark, fueling the cruelest nightmares. After surviving that hell, London hadn't allowed herself to imagine a future with any man. Now Collin was making her rethink what she had once refused to allow herself to ever believe in or hope for. He'd professed his love and every word of it had been like a sliver of light shining in the shade she'd taken shelter beneath. Her mother interrupted her thoughts.

"Your daddy and I really like him! And he's quite taken with you. He looks at you like you're the best thing since white bread!"

London laughed, "We're just friends, Mom."

"Okay. It's your lie. Tell it any way you want."

There was a moment of pause. London dropped her gaze to the tiled floor. "I'm scared." She lifted her eyes back to her mother, who had turned to stare at her. "I'm scared. Is that crazy?"

"You're scared of Collin? Has he hurt you? He hasn't hit you like Victor did, has he? Because if he has he'll need to leave this house right now! We're not going through that again, London." Her mother had bristled, ready to rage with indignation.

London shook her head vehemently. "No, nothing

like that. Collin's been incredible! I'm just afraid to trust that it won't blow up on me."

"Are you still seeing your therapist?"

"Not as often since I started seeing Collin."

Her mother hugged her tightly. "You need to keep doing the work, London. Your mental health is important."

"I know that."

"Good. I don't want your fear to get in the way of you living your life to the fullest. I don't want you missing out on what might be the single greatest experience of your lifetime because you're still fighting the ghosts of your past. That's why your father and I insisted on you seeing a therapist. It's why it's important that you have unbiased counsel to advise and guide you."

"I know, and I haven't stopped seeing the therapist. I've just been really happy and haven't needed to as much. That's all."

"Well, that says a lot about Mr. Stallion, then, doesn't it?"

"He's really incredible, Mom. He makes me laugh. He's attentive, generous, loving. He's pretty damn special!"

"And he makes you happy?"

"He really does!"

"Marry him! When you find a good man, grab him and hold on tight. Marry him!"

London laughed.

Her mother dropped down onto the wooden seat beside her. "Trust your intuition, London." She pressed her palm against her daughter's stomach. "Trust what you feel in your gut. You know if it's right. Just like you knew Victor wasn't right. Even before he became abusive, you knew! But you were desperate to have that happy ending even though you knew he wasn't your Prince Charming. Don't be scared to follow your heart if it feels right!"

Her mother leaned to kiss her cheek as she stood up and moved back to the oven, sliding the macaroni and cheese from inside. "Go tell the men to wash up for dinner. The food's ready to eat."

London nodded and stood up. She eased her way into the other room. Collin and her father were still sitting and enjoying the end of their movie, giggling like little boys. Amusement danced out of her eyes and lifted her lips in a full grin. She dropped down onto the sofa beside Collin. As she leaned into his side he wrapped his arms around her torso and hugged her tightly.

"Everything okay?" he asked.

She nodded. "Mom said for you two to come eat. The food's ready."

Her father practically jumped out of his seat. "Collin, my wife makes the best fried chicken this side of the Mississippi! It doesn't last long with this one home," he said as he gestured toward London, "so you better come on quick and get you some!"

Collin chuckled, "Yes, sir."

"We'll be right there, Daddy," London interjected.

She dropped a hand to Collin's thigh, stalling his trek to the dining room. He eyed her curiously.

Her father gave them both an all-knowing look. He nodded his head, blessing them with a warm smile. He pointed his index finger toward London. "I like this one. I think he's a keeper."

London grinned. "I think so, too, Daddy!" she exclaimed.

They watched as the patriarch headed toward the door, throwing them one last glance over his shoulder before disappearing out of the room.

"I really like your dad," Collin said. "In fact, both your parents are really great."

"They both like you, too."

"That's a good thing. I didn't want to be a disappointment to them. I know they have high expectations for the man who's going to marry you."

London laughed, "And you're going to be that man?"

"Of course. You're not planning on marrying anyone else, are you?"

She reached up to kiss his lips. "No. Something tells me you're going to be around for a good long while."

"That's what I told your dad."

"You did?"

Collin nodded. "When I told him I was in love with you."

"And what did he say?"

"He said I might want to give it some serious thought because you're just like your mother. Then he swirled his finger in a circle by his forehead. I think he was trying to warn me. But I told him I wasn't scared. That you were well worth the risk."

London rolled her eyes skyward, a soft chuckle easing past her lips. "I love you!" she exclaimed. "I really do love you!"

Collin grinned. "I know!" he said. He cupped his palm beneath her chin and kissed her lips. "I know!"

He hugged her again and pressed a damp kiss to her forehead. "So, are you ready to eat? I'm kind of hungry and your mom's chicken is smelling some sort of good!"

London laughed. "Let's go eat, then," she said.

Riding home from her parents', London couldn't help feeling like she'd won the lottery. A multi-million-dollar purse with a double-digit payout. Collin had her laughing with his corny jokes and stories about his past and family. She was giddy with joy, and for the first time in months, she felt like she'd finally found her way. Being with Collin felt like everything she trusted and believed in. It buoyed her confidence and had her flying like she was on cloud nine. He was the best memories and all the good times rolled up into the prettiest package with the biggest bow. He was love personified. He was home.

"People are going to think we're crazy. That we're rushing into things."

"Is that what they thought about your mom and dad when they married?"

"No. They thought mom and dad were crazy as hell! Who gets married after only knowing each other for three weeks?"

Collin laughed, "Then we're golden. It took you three weeks to have a civil conversation with me."

"I was not that bad… Well, not really… Okay, maybe a little. But I slept with you on our first date!"

"You did do that! And you did it very well if I may say so."

Laughter rang abundantly in the late-night air. They laughed and talked and laughed some more.

When they finally found their way back to London's apartment they were exhausted and ready for a good night's sleep. It was not lost on either of them that the following day was going to be long as they prepared for trial, ensuring they had left no detail unchecked.

Collin had already begun to doze when London stepped out of the bathroom after a quick shower. He lay across her bed, the towel from his own shower wrapped tightly around his waist. The sight of him made her smile, comfort coming in massive doses. She tapped him gently, hating to disturb his rest, but he only smiled as he crawled under the blankets, laid his head on a pillow and fell back to sleep.

Her phone rang, surprising her. She wasn't expecting anyone to be calling her at such a late hour. The display on the caller ID read Unknown. She pushed the button to reject the call and just seconds later it rang a second time. She waited and let it go to voice mail. When the indicator light flashed, she entered her code to access her messages and listened. Twenty-four seconds of breathing and then silence echoed over the phone line.

Shutting the device completely off, she turned to Collin, who had begun to snore softly. For reasons she would never be able to explain, his being there suddenly didn't have her feeling so at ease. Rising from the bed, she moved to check the locks and the alarm one more time.

Collin instinctively knew something was amiss. Something London wasn't eager to talk about. He cut an eye at her as they pulled out of the parking lot into traffic headed to work. She'd risen earlier than normal and was dressed and waiting when he rolled out of bed. She'd sat alone in her kitchen, a cup of coffee pressed between her palms. She'd looked lost and frustrated, her brow furrowed in thought.

"Good morning," he'd said, his singsong tone ringing loudly through the early-morning air.

London had barely given him a look, the faintest of smiles greeting him back. "We need to get moving," she'd answered. "I have a list of things I need to do to get ready for trial tomorrow."

"Would you like some breakfast?" he'd questioned as he moved to her side and kissed her cheek. "I make a mean omelet!"

London had shaken her head. "I'm not hungry. We just need to get going, please."

Despite his efforts to engage her, she'd been somber and distant, focused on something that was still weighing heavily on her spirit. After dressing quickly, they were out the door and headed toward the office.

He turned off the radio and silence filled the car. "What's wrong, London?"

She turned to look at him, the gesture abrupt as his question pulled her from her thoughts. "I'm sorry. I wasn't paying attention. What did you say?"

Collin chuckled softly, "I asked what's wrong with you. And don't tell me there's nothing the matter. Because I know something's not right. So, talk to me. Please!"

London blew a heavy sigh, the weight of it seeming to fill the interior of the car. Concern tinted his expression as his eyes shifted between the road and her.

"It's probably nothing..." she started.

"Let me decide that for myself."

She took a breath, then told him about the calls that had come in the night before.

"And no one was on the other end or left a message?"

She nodded. "And I know that doesn't sound like anything to be concerned about, that it was probably just a wrong number, but when I checked my phone this morning there were thirty-two missed calls and blank messages from that unknown number."

Collin nodded. "And you think it might be Victor Wells?"

There was a deafening pause. London hadn't wanted to say his name or give credence to the idea that Victor was once again stalking her. That he was back, determined to make her life miserable. That maybe he'd decided to make good on his claim to do her irreparable harm. She didn't want to believe it was Victor but she intuitively suspected Victor was knee-deep in the midst of it all. Something in her gut suddenly had her on guard and suspicious. She took another deep breath.

"I don't know. I just know it's odd," she finally said.

Collin fell into his own thoughts, not quite sure what to surmise from the situation. Clearly, it had London on edge, and that in and of itself had twisted a knot in his stomach. London being happy was foremost in his mind and if she had concerns, then so did he. He reached a hand out and wrapped his fingers around her forearm. He squeezed it gently, his touch heated and encouraging. "Let it go for now. I'll make some calls when we get to the office and see if we can find something out. Until we're certain, I don't want you to panic. Okay?"

London gave him the faintest smile. She wanted to trust him, to believe that he could make it all okay. She wanted to, but her history with Victor wouldn't let her. She pressed her hand against his. "I love you, Collin," she said softly.

Collin nodded. "I love you, too, London."

Once they were in the office, it was all hands on deck preparing for trial. Collin scrutinized all the state's evidence obtained during discovery. He reviewed the charging documents, police reports, lab tests and the witness statements. He made sure he hadn't missed anything, double-checking the detailed list of inconsistencies and wrongdoings he'd previously compiled. He and London studied the new evidence supplied by their independent investigators, reevaluating and verifying every known fact of the case. Despite having done the same things previously, neither was satisfied until the wealth of information was committed to memory.

By midafternoon they knew they were as prepared as they would ever be. Collin leaned back in his chair, his hands clasped behind his neck to alleviate the tension in his neck and shoulders. London had gone to the restroom, her menstrual cycle dropping a week early from the stress. While she was gone from the conference room, he slipped into his own office to make that call he'd promised.

Private investigator Vanessa Long answered on the third ring, her deep alto voice chiming warmly over the line. Vanessa had been a part of the Stallion family since Collin's father and uncles had been in elementary school. Best friends with his uncle Mark,

Vanessa and the Stallion clan had grown up together. For a brief moment, his uncle Mark and the woman had been boyfriend and girlfriend, the rest of the family thinking the two would end up together. College changed the dynamics of their relationship when Vanessa admitted her predilection for women. Each of the Stallion men had only been slightly disturbed when their family friend finally came out about her sexuality. But over time they had all found their balance, Vanessa acting as if she were just one of the boys and the Stallion men treating her so. The year Collin's parents had married, Vanessa had been pregnant with her son, Vaughan. She'd been a single mother running one of the most successful private investigation firms in the state. The Stallions often utilized her services for business, trusting her efforts whenever they were needed.

"Long and Associates. This is Vanessa."

"Aunt Vanessa, hey. It's Collin."

"Collin? Hey, baby! How are you? Where are you? What's wrong?"

Collin laughed, "Nothing's wrong. I'm calling you from work actually," he said as he gave her a quick update on what he'd been up to since returning home from college.

"That's why you should call me more often. I don't hear from you for months and I immediately get nervous."

"Sorry about that. The reason I'm calling, though, is I could use your help."

"Whatever you need, baby! Tell me what's going on."

It took a few short minutes to update the woman,

briefly detailing London's history with her ex and her concerns about the unknown calls. Vanessa listened, and Collin knew she was taking notes, jotting everything she deemed important on a yellow-lined legal pad.

"What's her cell phone number?" Vanessa asked.

Collin recited the ten-digit number. As he did, London passed his door and gestured for his attention. He cupped his palm over the phone receiver.

"You about ready to leave?"

He nodded. "Give me one more minute."

London nodded and turned back toward the conference room. He went back to his conversation. Vanessa was repeating the phone number, verifying she'd gotten it right.

"That's correct."

"Let me do some digging. And do me a favor."

"What's that?"

"Tell your friend not to go home for a few days. Just to be safe."

"You think she might have a problem?"

"I think it's better to be safe than sorry. Men who are abusive are nothing to play around with. If he's been as violent toward her as she alleges, then that means he's unpredictable."

"Okay, I'll make sure she stays safe."

His aunt chuckled, noting the concern in his tone. "It's like that, is it? My, my, my! I can't wait to meet this friend of yours! You know she'll have to pass my approval, right?"

Collin laughed, "I think you'll like her. She's pretty special."

"I'm sure I will. I'll give you a call as soon as

I have some information. Until then, you two keep yourselves safe."

"We will. Thank you."

Collin disconnected the call. He cleared his desk and reached for his briefcase. He was headed back to the conference room when a commotion rang through the office. Felicia was hurrying from the other direction, followed by a delivery person carrying a large bouquet of flowers. There was a moment of amusement until he realized there were ten delivery people in total, each juggling two or three floral arrangements, each one larger than the other. He and the flower people walked into the room at the same time.

The look on London's face was chilling. The color had drained from her face and she'd begun to shake. Tears misted her eyes and there was no missing that she was petrified. He moved swiftly to her side, shielding her from view, as Felicia gushed excitedly about the delivery.

"London, they say all these flowers are for you! Who sent you flowers?" she asked as she went searching for a note card. "This is amazing!"

Collin cupped her face in his hands as the first tears rained over her cheeks. "Let's go," he commanded, his voice low. "It's going to be fine."

"It's Victor," she whispered, clutching the front of his shirt. "He's going to kill me!"

Collin shook his head. "Hold it together, baby. Victor isn't going to do anything. Trust me!"

London met the intense stare he was giving her. She didn't have a clue how long they stood together, staring at each other, but his gaze was soothing, and she instantly felt her anxiety beginning to lift. She nodded her head. "Okay," she said as she took two deep inhales of air. "I'm okay."

Collin nodded. He swiped the tears from her face, and when he was certain she'd regained control of her emotions, he stepped to the side. He turned and gave Felicia the brightest smile he could muster.

The woman eyed the two of them curiously.

London rolled her eyes skyward. "Attorney Stallion has quite the sense of humor," she said. "He's already celebrating our win and we haven't made it to court yet."

"You sent her flowers?" Felicia asked.

Collin laughed, "I'm good like that!"

"Aw, sookie sookie, now!" she said, a cheesy grin filling her face.

"Leave it alone, Felicia," London chimed.

"I just want to know if this means you two are official. Because Paula and I know you've been seeing each other. Even when you were denying it, we knew."

"It means," London said as she swept by her friend and headed to the door, "that Mr. Stallion is quite the force to be reckoned with."

"I know that's right," Felicia said, her arms folded over her chest as she looked him up and down.

"Attorney Stallion and I are gone for the rest of the day," London said. "We're going straight to the courthouse in the morning. Just call my cell phone if anyone needs us," she said.

Felicia nodded. She reached to give London a hug. "Knock 'em dead tomorrow. You've got this. Oh, and Perry asked me to tell you that he will meet you two in the morning. He had a board meeting this afternoon, so he didn't come in today."

London hugged her friend back. "Thank you."

"Oh, and here. There was one card, although you probably don't need it now, right?"

London winced ever so slightly as she took the note card and pushed it into the pocket of her slacks. "Thanks."

Felicia pointed her finger at Collin. "Take care of my friend or we will hurt you!"

Paula suddenly rushed into the room. "Who's hurting who? And where did all these flowers come from?"

"Girl!" Felicia exclaimed to their bestie as she waved goodbye to the couple. "Do I have some tea for you!"

Chapter 11

After a quick trip to her apartment to throw some clothes into a small suitcase, Collin and London headed to his house. While she was packing, Collin had called Vanessa to tell her about the floral delivery. Now he sat, twisting the note card in his hands, ire rising slowly from the pit of his stomach.

The card had been printed in bold black ink. Three threatening lines. "I have a bullet with Stallion's name on it. Yours, too. I have my eye on you." He'd read it over and over again, not at all amused. His aunt Vanessa hadn't been thrilled by it either, admonishing him to be careful. Now he debated whether or not to tell his parents.

London came out of the bathroom, stopping short when she spied him. They locked gazes as he stood up and slid the card into his back pocket. She sighed, a heavy gust of air rushing past her lips.

"He always sent flowers before he beat me," she said. "He got some sort of perverse thrill out of it. How many he sent and how bad the beating would be depended on what I'd done. One bouquet, and maybe it would only be a few slaps. Large bouquets meant the beating would be worse."

"He's not going to hurt you, London. I won't let that happen."

London moved into his arms, wrapping her arms around his waist. He hugged her, and she held on as if her life depended on it, because in some ways it did. There was an abrupt knock on the front door and his brother, Jake, suddenly screamed his name, interrupting the moment.

London laughed as she took a step back. Collin shook his head. He grabbed her hand and pulled her back to the living room. The guesthouse was a spacious twelve-hundred-square-foot cottage with hardwoods and an open floor plan. It had a sizable chef's kitchen with forty-two-inch cherry cabinets and stainless steel appliances. Double ovens, a gas cooktop, tile backsplash and a wealth of counter space made it highly desirable. There was also a double-sided fireplace between the living room and dining area. The oversize master suite featured a tray ceiling, and a large sitting area framed by pillars that he used as a home office. There were large walk-in closets and the master bath featured a massive soaking tub and a separate glass-and-tile shower with a sitting bench. A second bedroom and large bath completed the floor plan.

By the time Collin reached the door Jake was letting himself inside. "Collin!"

"Hey, bud, why are you screaming?"

"Hey!" Jake leaned to peer past his big brother, waving at London excitedly. "Mom says to come to the house. Aunt Vanessa is here and needs to talk to you."

Collin's eyes widened. "Aunt Vanessa?"

"And Uncle Mark, Uncle John, Uncle Mason and Uncle Luke and everybody. It's like Sunday breakfast. Everyone is here!"

Collin cussed. He tossed a look over his shoulder. Keeping what was going on under wraps was no longer an option. The impromptu family meeting meant his parents already knew. And so did the rest of the Stallion family.

Jake laughed, "You said *fuck*!"

"Don't you swear!" Collin admonished. "I shouldn't have said it. And don't you tell Mom!"

Jake shook his head vehemently. "It's cool. Me and London can keep a secret. Right, London?"

"We sure can, Jake!" she said. She sauntered past Collin and extended her hand toward the boy. "Will you walk me to the house, please?"

"Sure!" he said as he took her hand, swinging her arm between them. "I'd show you the shortcut, but we'd have to go through the bushes. You're a girl, so we'll go the long way."

"We will not! I know how to cut through some bushes!" she exclaimed.

Jake grinned. "I like you! I wish my girlfriend was cool like you!"

"Race you!" London said as she tagged him on the shoulder and took off running.

Jake tore after her, laughing hysterically. "Last one there's a rotten egg, Collin!"

Laughing with them, Collin jumped down the steps, debating how far he planned to let them get ahead before he closed the distance and passed the two of them.

As the trio entered the home, they found the family seated around the dining room table. Conversation stopped midsentence as everyone inside turned to stare. The moment was suddenly awkward. The look on Katrina Stallion's face spoke volumes—the matriarch was clearly not happy. London suddenly found herself wishing for a deep hole to crawl into.

Matthew spoke first, breaking the silence that had fallen over the room. "Jake, you and Vaughan head up to your room, please."

Collin turned, noticing the other boy for the first time. Only a few months older than Jake, Vaughan Long stood a good six inches taller and some forty pounds heavier.

"Vaughan, hey!" Collin said, greeting the kid warmly. The two slapped palms and bumped shoulders. "You're almost taller than I am!"

Vaughan gave him a silver-plated smile, a mouthful of braces catching the light. "Mom taught me how to drive," the kid said. "Maybe you can take me driving?"

Vanessa cleared her throat. "Uh, no! You have to have an adult with you and be in your teens to drive legally. Or did you forget?"

"He is an adult," Vaughan replied. "With a Mercedes!"

Collin gave the woman a look. "Really, Aunt Vanessa? You're going to do me like that?"

She shrugged. "An adult over fifty!"

Mark laughed, "Leave my godsons alone, please. We got this. I swear, you women do your sons a serious disservice the way you're constantly babying them."

Vanessa cut an evil eye at her best friend. "Excuse me?"

"I'm serious. A woman cannot raise a boy to be a man when you're always worrying about them breaking. They need to fall down and tear things up every now and again. All you want to do is spoil and coddle and pamper them so they grow up looking for some other woman to take care of them."

John and Matthew were nodding their agreement, wide grins filling their dark faces. Vanessa moved to Katrina's side, both women eyeing them with narrowed stares and arms crossed over their chests.

Vanessa changed the subject. "We'll finish this conversation at the next Sunday breakfast, Mark Stallion. I have some things to say but I'm going to hold my tongue for the moment. Vaughan, you and Jake disappear, please, so we can have a conversation. And maybe, if it's okay with Aunt Katrina and Uncle Matthew, Jake can go home with us tonight and you two can go to school together in the morning."

"I can spend the night?" Jake asked excitedly.

Katrina gave him a look. "It will all depend on how long it takes you two to go upstairs to your room."

The loud pounding of the two boys racing up the

steps echoed through the home. The adults laughed, heads shaking at the two of them.

Katrina gestured toward London and Collin with her head. "Why don't you two come sit down?" she said softly. "Vanessa was just filling us in on everything that's going on."

London suddenly felt like crying. "I'm so sorry, Judge Stallion. I never wanted my personal problems to touch Collin, or your family."

"Oh, no! Sweetheart! You have nothing to apologize for!" Katrina exclaimed. She rose from her seat and wrapped her arms around the young woman's shoulders. "We just want to make sure you're both safe right now. That's our only concern."

Collin reached into his back pocket and handed Vanessa the note card. He watched as she read it once, then a second time. She tossed him a look before passing it to Matthew. No one spoke as it slowly made its way around the room. It stopped at Mark last and he slammed it against the table, his anger simmering.

"That fool is going to make someone hurt him," Mark snapped. "I will bust him dead in his face!"

John shook his head. "That's not going to happen. We all have too much to lose."

"I still can't believe it," Luke said. "I met him at some fund-raiser last year and he seemed like a decent guy."

"I'd heard rumors," Katrina interjected, "but I never knew how to take them other than they were just that…rumors."

"I knew he could be aggressive," Matthew said, recalling an experience at a dinner where he'd given a waitperson a hard time. "I'd also heard him espouse his philosophy about women and relationships, and I'd dismissed it as nothing but talk."

Vanessa shook her head. "Well, it's more than that. From what little I was able to dig up, he's been accused of some pretty wretched behavior, and was always able to get ahead of it. From what I gather he's been able to use fear and intimidation to keep his victims silent. One woman apparently left everything—friends, family, business, *everything*—to get away from him."

"He's got everyone fooled," London said, her voice a loud whisper. "Most think he's this upstanding citizen and he's truly a monster in sheep's clothing."

They all listened as London detailed the horrors Victor Wells had put her through. She spilled every detail, the violence, betrayal, the fear. When she finished, the emotion was at an all-time high, everyone in the room suddenly on edge.

"Well, that's some low-level bullshit," Mark snapped. "You don't beat a woman and you don't ever put your hands on a Stallion woman! No one threatens ours!"

London was shaking, unable to look any of them in the eye for fear she would start crying the ugly cry. Collin wrapped his arms around her and pulled her close. "So, what do we do?" he questioned.

"The Jerome James trial starts tomorrow, correct?" Matthew asked.

London and Collin both nodded.

"You ready?" his father asked.

"Yes, sir, we're more than prepared."

"I can put a private security detail on the two of them," Vanessa said.

"I don't think…" Collin started.

Vanessa held up a hand to stall his comment. "You won't even know they're there. Right now, we don't have enough to legally go after him. We can't get a restraining order until he does something."

"He's too smart for that," Collin said.

"He's not that smart," Matthew concluded. "He's leaving messages and sending flowers. Something's got him riled up. He'll make a mistake."

Clarity suddenly washed over Collin's face. "I petitioned a case review with the state, alleging prosecutorial misconduct. Justice Wells was the lead prosecutor on the original case. I'm sure he's recently received notice."

John gave his nephew a smile. "Sounds like you poked a bear!"

"I just did my job, sir."

Matthew's stare was filled with pride. He gave his son a slight nod. "Arrange for that security detail, Vanessa. Let's see what happens over the next few days and go from there."

Katrina ordered pizza for dinner, the family's focus shifting to topics more positive. In no time at all they were all bonding over pizza, beer, salad and potato chips. Collin and London excused themselves early, needing to rest up for the next day. Mark and John were still knee-deep in conversation with Collin's parents when Collin and London exited out the back door and returned to the guesthouse.

"So, what's your pretrial ritual?" he asked as he poured them both a glass of moscato that he'd swiped from his parents' refrigerator. He unwrapped the slices of pound cake his mother had sent with them.

"I always wear something red. It's my power color. The night before, I sometimes binge-watch horror movies until I fall asleep. I just try to relax, and in the morning, I'll take a walk and rehearse my opening statement or any key legal argument I need to make during trial."

"Horror movies relax you?"

London shrugged. "I like horror movies! What about you? What are your rituals?"

"The night before, I usually read to unwind. Then in the mornings I might go horseback riding."

"So, what do you read? What kind of books do you like?"

"Biographies and memoirs, mostly. I also enjoy a good history book."

"No fiction?"

"The last fiction book I read was Guy Johnson's *Standing at the Scratch Line*. You might enjoy that. It's a historical romance of sorts. The book is on my desk, if you're interested."

London took a bite of her cake. "I'll have to check it out."

"I'll tell you what. Why don't we soak in a hot tub, then crawl into bed? You can control the television remote, then in the morning we'll go over to the ranch and ride."

"Will we have time?"

"I'll call over and ask them to saddle up two of the horses before we get there. We can ride for an hour, then come back and shower. I'll make sure we get up early enough so that we won't feel rushed." Collin took a sip of his wine and washed down the last bite of sweet cake.

London leaned her head on his shoulder. "Your family was very sweet to me."

"My family likes you. They also know how much you mean to me. They're not going to let anyone mess with a future Mrs. Stallion. You heard my uncle."

"*Mrs*. Stallion!"

"Personally, I kind of like the sound of that. How about you?"

London shrugged. "Mrs. Jacobs *hyphen* Stallion sounds better."

Collin laughed, "Whatever you want, baby, as long as it sounds like you're all mine!"

London settled herself down between Collin's legs as he wrapped himself around her. She leaned back against his broad chest. The heated bathwater lapped warmly around them. Collin hugged her tightly as she thanked him again for what he and his family were doing for her. "I can't begin to tell you how much I appreciate the support you've all shown me," she said as he leaned to kiss her forehead.

"You will always be able to trust that my family will be here for you. Always."

She reached to kiss his lips, then allowed herself to relax for the first time in a good long while. The two breathed in sync with each other, and every so often a soft moan or a light whimper would escape from one of them. He leaned and kissed her neck, whispering into her ear. "You are so beautiful," he said, moving his mouth back to her mouth as he kissed her hungrily.

A firm hand ventured into London's nether regions, slick moisture dampening his fingers. He continued to kiss her, his hands teasing and taunting her femininity with exact precision. An orgasm suddenly shook London to her core, the sensation jolting her into reverie. Before she could catch her breath, Collin scooped her up into his arms and carried her to his bed. He sheathed himself with a condom and eased his body into hers. His strokes were slow and controlled, gaining in momentum as London moaned with each thrust. Collin found himself lost in her, completely abandoned in everything he loved about London.

She pushed against him, meeting him stroke for stroke, harder and harder. London had missed his touch without even knowing it, and he hers, and they loved each other as if they might not ever be able to make love to each other again. Collin savored the sensation of hot wet velvet wrapped tightly around him and when his orgasm erupted it was powerful and loud as he screamed out with pleasure, London unrelenting in her ministrations. As his body spewed in pleasure, London shrieked his name over and over, her nails digging into the flesh along his back. Between them the air was thick and heavy, and both felt as though they might never catch their breath.

London gasped as she pressed herself beneath him, holding on tightly. She nuzzled her face into his neck, lightly lapping at the salty perspiration that moistened his flesh. Their joy was epic and all either wanted was for it to go on for eternity.

"Are you okay?" Collin whispered, hugging her tightly.

London nodded her face against his chest. "Better than okay," she answered. "I feel incredible." And then they both drifted off into a deep sleep.

Chapter 12

Entering the courtroom, Collin wasn't surprised to find his family seated in the galley. His parents sat side by side, with John and Mark seated together in the row behind them. They all greeted the two of them with a nod.

He and London were talking to the bailiff, waiting for the jailer to bring Mr. James to the courtroom, when Victor Wells swooped into the room. His arrival was quite the production as he greeted the prosecutor like they were two old friends. He made as if to move toward London when Collin stepped between them.

"Justice Wells," he said, his curt tone short and to the point.

"Attorney Stallion."

"I'm glad to see you got my invitation. Wasn't sure

if you'd show up. Cowards usually run when they're put on the spot."

Victor bristled. "You're playing in the big leagues now, Stallion. I will destroy you."

"I'm sure you'll try."

"It's going to be a shame to see your career crash and burn so soon."

Collin took a step closer to the man, his voice dropping an octave as he whispered under his breath, "Stay away from London. If you know what's good for you, you'll forget you ever knew her."

Victor whispered back, "I'm not going away. You don't know who you're messing with. She broke my rules and I won't be done until she's been punished. And you, little boy, will just be collateral damage." The judge smiled, doing an about-face as he settled himself on a front pew. His expression was smug, and it took everything in Collin not to punch him in his face.

As he turned, Collin caught his father's eye. Matthew was staring at him intently. Collin tossed him a smile. Theirs was a silent conversation that passed briefly, something between father and son that only they understood. Collin gave him one last nod as he moved to the defense table.

London was standing there watching the room, fighting to contain her anxiety. The color had drained from her face and she was visibly struggling to keep herself standing, her knees shaking with fear. She was holding tight to the table with one hand, the other balled into a tight fist at her side. Under her breath she was muttering to herself, "Keep it together. Keep it together. Keep it together."

She shot Victor a narrowed glare before focusing her attention on Collin. He picked up a folder from the table and leaned against her. They huddled close to each other, feigning interest in the paperwork in his hands.

"How are you holding up?" he asked her softly.

"I've been better. He said something to you, didn't he?"

"He's just trying to throw us off our game."

"Well, it's working."

"Don't you worry. Focus on the case. That's our priority. Let's prove he screwed our client over. Let's make Justice Wells regret getting out of bed this morning!"

London smiled and nodded. "Okay," she said. "We can do this!"

"Damn Skippy!" he responded.

London laughed as he pulled out her chair and held it for her. She took a seat, folding her hands atop the table to wait.

Jerome James's arrival was met with a low burst of noise and a rise of energy throughout the wood-paneled room. He was clearly happy to see his son and family, and for the first time since knowing him, Collin sensed a hint of nervousness in the man's demeanor as he shook the elder's hand.

"Good morning, sir."

"Good morning, young man. Mighty pretty day outside."

Collin smiled. 'Yes, sir, it is."

"Try your best to keep it that way, please."

"Yes, sir," Collin said with a soft chuckle.

Minutes later the bailiff called for everyone in the

room to stand. The judge, the Honorable Liza Montenegro, entered the room, swept her robes beneath her and took a seat. The bailiff then called the courtroom to order.

Collin suddenly jotted something on the notepad in front of him. He slid the note past Mr. James toward London. As she read the words *I love you; now, kick butt*, printed in bold letters, a smile swept across her face, and she nodded. Mr. James grinned, looking from one to the other.

"Yes, sir," he muttered. "A really pretty day!"

"Is the prosecution ready?" Judge Montenegro asked.

"Yes, your honor," the prosecutor answered.

The judge turned her gaze toward the defense table. "I have a motion before me to dismiss all charges against your client, Jerome James. Is that correct, Ms. Jacobs?"

London rose to her feet. "It is, Your Honor."

The prosecutor stood up, as well. "Your Honor, Mr. James's original conviction was recently set aside, and he has been granted a new trial. The defense has nothing to substantiate their request for all charges to be dropped. This is clearly a waste of the court's time."

"That is untrue, Your Honor. The defense is prepared to show beyond any reasonable doubt that our client was wrongly charged and should never have been convicted. We're prepared to show that the state purposely withheld viable evidence in Mr. James's initial case that would have completely exonerated him."

The judge paused, seeming to drop into reflection. She finally nodded her head. "Proceed, Counselor. Let's see what you have."

"Thank you, Your Honor."

For the next fifteen minutes, London succinctly presented the case they'd spent weeks laying out. She introduced all the newly discovered evidence. CODIS, the DNA database system, had identified the unknown male DNA profile from the semen in the Jameses' marital bed and the bloody towel discovered in the woods behind the home. It was a perfect match for a convicted felon named Robert Palmer. Palmer, originally a native of New Mexico, had a lengthy criminal record in five states and had been living in Texas at the time of Mary James's murder. He was also a perfect match to hair fibers recovered at the scene of the crime. And a perfect match to hair fibers found at the murders of six other women bludgeoned to death in the same manner as Mary James while her husband was in prison. Robert Palmer was currently doing three life sentences in the state of Arizona.

She introduced the eyewitness testimony of Mr. James's son, who'd been adamant that his father had not been home at the time of the murder, and his detailed description of the bad man who had hurt his mother. He had described perfectly Robert Palmer's facial scar and eye deformity. London successfully entered into evidence every document from the prosecution's files confirming Jerome James's innocence that had been withheld at trial.

She moved back to the table to check the last of her notes. The prosecution was arguing to have some of the evidence excluded. Collin gestured for her attention and she leaned across the table as he whispered in her ear. She stepped back and stared at him, a question mark on her face.

Collin nodded his head slowly until she gave him a look of agreement.

"Objection," London suddenly called out to something the prosecutor was saying out of turn.

"Sustained," Judge Montenegro said. "Do you have anything else, Ms. Jacobs?"

"Yes, Your Honor. We'd like to call a witness to the stand."

The prosecutor jumped from his seat. "Objection, Your Honor, we never received a witness list."

London passed a document to the judge and a copy to the prosecutor. "Extenuating circumstances, Your Honor. The subpoena was only issued last night, and we weren't sure it would be served in time for the witness to be here. I'd ask the court for a little leeway."

"Objection overruled. Considering the circumstances of this case I'll allow you some latitude, Ms. Jacobs. Proceed accordingly."

"Thank you, Your Honor. The defense calls Justice Victor Wells to the stand."

Justice Wells stood slowly, adjusting and then buttoning his suit jacket around his torso. His movements were slow and deliberate as he sauntered to the witness stand. Before he took his seat, the bailiff asked him to raise his right hand and to place his left on a copy of the King James Bible.

"Do you solemnly swear to tell the truth, the whole truth and nothing but the truth, so help you God?"

He nodded. "I do."

"Please, have a seat."

As Victor moved to sit down, he gave London a wry smile, winking at her. She turned abruptly, moving back to the defense table and her chair. Collin slowly stood up, flipping through a few papers before he moved to stand in front of the witness stand. Justice Wells's smug expression dropped, confusion washing over his face.

"Good morning, Justice Wells. We apologize for any inconvenience. We appreciate you taking time out of your busy schedule for us." Collin was cordial, his tone almost buoyant. Gone was the attitude from earlier.

Victor crossed his arms over his chest. "Not a problem."

"Would you please state your full name for the record?"

"Victor Harrison Wells."

"And you have been licensed to practice law in the state of Texas since 1986, is that correct?"

"Yes."

"Would you tell the court what your current employment position is, please?"

Justice Wells took a breath, annoyance furrowing his brow. "I was recently nominated and elected to the Texas Supreme Court."

"Thank you, Justice Wells. Now, prior to your current appointment, you were employed by the city of Dallas, where you've served as the chief prosecutor for the state, is that correct?"

"Yes."

"You were the senior prosecutor in the Jerome James case, is that correct?"

"Yes."

"Do you recall, sir, who the primary police investigator was for the case?

Victor shrugged his shoulders. "I don't recall."

Collin moved to the desk and retrieved a document London held out for him. "Maybe this will help jog your memory," he said as he passed the paper to the judge. "Your Honor, this is the original police report presented to the prosecutor's office. It's already been entered into evidence, labeled exhibit number seven."

The judge nodded, pulling her copy of the document from the stack of papers on the podium.

"Justice Wells, can you now tell us who the lead investigator was, please?"

"Detective Hiram Moore."

"And whose decision was it to not call Detective Moore to the stand during Mr. James's original trial? Was that your decision?"

"I don't recall."

"Do you by chance recall why the decision was made?"

"Detective Moore's testimony was deemed irrelevant to the outcome of the case."

"Despite his being the lead investigator with significant proof that the defendant might not have been guilty?"

"Young man, get to your point."

"Answer the question, please," Judge Montenegro chastised, giving him side-eye.

"As I said, we didn't feel his testimony was needed or substantial."

"Whose decision was it to withhold that information from the defense?"

"I don't recall."

"But you were the lead prosecutor?"

"Yes." His response was terse, a hint of anger rising in his tone.

"Justice Wells, who is Brenda James?"

"Excuse me?"

"Brenda James. What is your relationship to Brenda James?"

Justice Wells suddenly turned a significant shade of red, color like a spotlight on each cheek. "I don't recall."

"Let me jog your memory. Brenda James is the sister of Jerome James. Prosecution records show she spoke to you numerous times about her brother's case. Is that correct?"

"Objection, Your Honor. Hearsay!"

"Overruled. Answer the question, Justice Wells."

"Maybe, I'm not sure."

"In fact, sir, you pursued Miss James, wanting a romantic relationship. Isn't that true?"

"Objection, Your Honor. Relevance?" The prosecutor shot Collin a dirty look, suddenly looking like he was going to be sick.

"Overruled. Where is this going, Counselor?"

"If you'll bear with me, Your Honor, I assure you, I'll get to my point quickly."

The judge nodded. "Proceed."

"Your Honor, I'd like to enter into evidence this police report dated two weeks after Mr. James's arrest. It's a statement taken by detective Hiram Moore from Brenda James."

Collin passed documents to the judge and the other attorney. He also gave a copy to Victor.

The judge nodded. "So entered."

"Justice Wells, would you please read the highlighted portion of the statement taken by your lead detective on this case for the court?"

Justice Wells read the document to himself first, his color darkening another two shades of crimson. He suddenly stammered, "I... It... W-well..."

"Let me help you out," Collin said. "The complainant, Miss Brenda James, states that Victor Wells, the prosecuting attorney on her brother's murder charge, approached her about being able to help secure her brother's freedom. He stated that in exchange for a sexual favor the charges would go away. When she rebuffed his advances, she was physically assaulted, suffering multiple bruises and contusions. She also stated that she'd told her story to a local sheriff, the Dallas police and staff at the hospital, but no one believed her."

Victor snapped, "That was a damn lie! There was no proof, and no charges were ever filed against me."

"No, there weren't. In fact, detective Moore buried this police report at your request. Isn't that true?"

Victor's face twisted in a harsh snarl. "Watch yourself, Counselor. Do you know who I am?"

"Justice Wells, just answer the questions you're asked, please," Judge Montenegro admonished.

"Justice Wells, is it true that detective Moore was hired by the prosecutor's office on your recommendation to be a senior investigator reporting directly to you?"

"I don't recall."

"Do you recall that his appointment with a starting salary of forty-two thousand dollars happened exactly one week after Brenda James filed her report?"

"I know what you're trying to imply, and you will not..." Victor started, his jaw locked tight with hostility.

"I have no further questions, Your Honor," Collin interrupted.

"You may step down, Justice Wells," the presiding justice stated.

Everyone watched as Victor Wells rose from where he sat, stepping down out of the witness box. Stonefaced, he crossed the room and exited the courtroom, not bothering to look back.

Collin moved back to the table, pulling another document into his hands. "Your Honor, I'd like to also enter into evidence a copy of the formal complaint made against Justice Wells and the prosecutor's office. Yesterday afternoon the Texas Supreme Court ordered a formal court of inquiry to determine whether or not Victor Wells committed misconduct in Jerome James's original case."

"I've heard enough," Judge Montenegro stated. "Counselors, I want to see you both in my chambers," she ordered as she stood up and grabbed her files. "The court is taking a brief recess," she said.

The bailiff yelled out, "All rise!"

Collin and London locked gazes. Both tried to remain stoic despite knowing that the interrogation had been successful. The bailiff gestured for them to follow, the judge waiting in her office to be heard. She stood with her arms crossed, leaning against her desk. She directed her comments toward the prosecutor.

"Mr. Denver, we have a dilemma. So, before I render my verdict, I'd like to ask, based on the evidence presented, how you would like to proceed?"

London and Collin stared at the man, anticipation like an electric current firing in the early-afternoon air.

He blew a sigh of defeat. "Your Honor, the state of

Texas would like to drop all charges and extend an apology to Mr. James."

"That's what I thought. The court accepts your decision." She gave Matthew and London a look. "Congratulations. Your client was well served. It was an honor to have you both in my courtroom today."

"Thank you, Your Honor!" the two chimed in unison.

Thirty minutes later, Judge Montenegro slammed the gavel down, declaring Jerome James a free man. The courtroom erupted in cheers. Tears rained from London's eyes as she hugged Mr. James, his appreciation ringing loudly in her ears, the man sobbing with sheer joy. In the back of the courtroom Collin's parents and uncles were hugging each other tightly, pride gleaning over their faces.

Perry waved for Collin's attention, reaching over the gallery railing to shake his hand. "Nice job, Stallion. Chalk one up for justice!"

"Thank you, sir."

"The press is going to want a statement from all of you. We'll try to keep it short and sweet, so Mr. James can go home to be with his family. He can decide in the next week or so if he's interested in doing any lengthy interviews."

The two men turned to watch as Mr. James hugged his people, clinging to his son and daughter, who were both crying like babies.

London had moved to Collin's side, grabbing his arm. "Congratulations," she whispered.

"I'm very proud of you," Collin replied. "We make a great team!"

"I know that's right." She smiled sweetly.

Collin wrapped his arms around her and hugged her tightly. "You ready to talk to the press?"

She took a breath. "As ready as I'll ever be."

"Just remember," Perry interjected, "you have no comment about the pending review against Justice Wells. Is that understood?"

They both nodded. Clearing the table, they packed the assortment of files into their briefcases. They watched as Perry followed after Mr. James, the bailiff taking him to retrieve his personal possessions and be processed out of the system. They held hands as they exited the courtroom. When they were alone in the elevator, Collin pulled her into his arms and kissed her boldly. In that moment, everything between them was perfection.

Riding down to the first floor, she clutched his arm. In the lobby, they stood side by side, leaning casually against each other. They waited for Mr. James and Perry to finish the paperwork. When the two men stepped out of the elevator, Jerome James walked with a renewed air of confidence. He was suddenly like a ray of light with a fresh bulb.

"Mr. James would like to go straight home with his son," Perry said. "It's been a long day for him and he'd like to rest. We've arranged for him to come into the office on Thursday to talk to Paula about the benefits available to him, so she can make the necessary arrangements. I've invited him to a celebratory dinner with the firm right after. I trust you'll both be there."

"We wouldn't miss it," London said.

Collin nodded. He extended his arm to shake Mr. James's hand. "Congratulations, sir!"

"You did good today, son. You kept that sun shining down on me."

"I was determined to keep my promise, Mr. James."

He nodded. "I trust I'll get me an invitation to that wedding?"

Collin laughed, "You have my word, sir. We won't do it without you there."

Jerome slapped him warmly against the back and then headed toward the front door.

On the steps of the Frank Crowley Courts Building London thanked the judge, the prosecutor and the staff of the Pro Bono Partnership of Dallas for their service. Collin asked that the media respect their client's privacy as he assimilated himself back into society. Mr. James expressed his appreciation to everyone who'd believed in his innocence and had supported him during his incarceration.

When the fanfare was done and finished, all questions asked that could be answered, Jerome James said his goodbyes and climbed into his son's black SUV. Perry gave them one last round of accolades and ordered them to take some time off to clear their heads and prepare for the next case waiting for attention. Waving goodbye, Collin and London bypassed the office celebration and headed home.

Chapter 13

London was still sleeping soundly, sprawled across both sides of Collin's bed. For reasons he couldn't explain, Collin was restless, sleep eluding him. He had tossed and turned until he'd grown weary of staring at the ceiling. He had tried to read, but was unable to focus on the words on his Kindle and then he had paced the living room floor until he grew weary of walking.

As he dressed, slipping into a pair of gray sweatpants and a T-shirt, he was careful not to disturb London's rest. He knew it had been a while since she'd last rested well. Exhaustion had finally caught up with her and he was glad that she felt safe enough to fully relax.

Collin cut through the bushes to the main house. He tiptoed through the back door, easing it open and then closing it slowly. He moved right to the refrigerator, excited when he spotted leftover chicken and dumplings in a Tupperware container. He'd just taken the bowl from the microwave oven and made himself comfortable on a kitchen stool when the overhead lights in the room were switched on. His mother greeted him with a bright smile.

"I thought I heard someone down here rummaging through my refrigerator. I was just about to give your little brother a hard time."

Collin smiled back. "Sorry. I was trying to be quiet about my breaking and entering."

"Where's London?"

"Sleeping. She was exhausted."

"We were so proud of you two. You did an excellent job."

"Those take-your-kid-to-work days paid off!" he said with a little laugh.

Katrina laughed with him. She moved to the fridge and poured herself a small glass of cranberry juice. She grabbed a bag of chocolate-chip cookies from the cupboard and moved to the counter to sit with him.

"So, what's got you all wound up?"

Collin shrugged his shoulders as he swallowed a spoonful of chicken. "I keep thinking about Justice Wells coming after London and what I would do if anything happens to her."

"You care about her a lot, don't you?"

"I love her. I'm *in* love with her. And I know you think it's too soon and I'm too young, but…"

Katrina held up her hand, stalling his last words. "No, actually I don't think that at all. You forget, I was nineteen when I fell in love with your father and not much older than that when we had you."

"How did you know? With both my dads? How did you know?"

"I just knew. They both came in and swept me off my feet. Both were overly romantic and exceptionally protective, and, well, it just felt right. With Jackson, he was that first love with the butterflies and those first-time experiences. With Matthew, I just instinctively knew that he would be my last love. It was just something I felt inside," she said, tapping at her heart.

Collin nodded. "Well, I love her, Mom. I didn't think it was possible to love someone as much as I love London. But she's all I can think about and I don't know if I could take it if anything happened to her. I think that's why Justice Wells has been on my mind."

Katrina dropped her hand against the back of his. "I don't think you need to worry about Wells and if he tries anything, you have some pretty powerful people behind you. Trust that. Your father and your uncles would never let anything happen to you or London."

Collin pondered her words for a moment. Just the hum of the refrigerator and the occasional clank of the ice maker dropping ice sounded through the air. He lifted his eyes back to his mother, taking a breath before he spoke again. "It's important to me that you like her, Mom. I don't think I could take it if the two women I love more than anything else in this world didn't like each other."

Katrina smiled. "Actually, what I know about London, I like very much. She's intelligent, beautiful, and she loves my baby boy. I can see it when she looks at you. She loves you and she makes you happy. And all I have ever wanted is for you to be happy. I'm sure that as she and I get to know each other better, I will like her even more." She pressed a warm palm to the side of his face.

"Thank you," Collin said with a bright smile. "I guess I should head back to bed and try to get some sleep."

"Before you go, I have something for you," Katrina said as she slid off the stool. "Don't leave!"

She exited the room, the quiet slipping back in to take her place. Collin finished the last spoonful of chicken and dumplings. Rising, he moved to the sink to rinse his bowl and put it into the dishwasher.

Katrina moved swiftly back into the room. She carried a small black box. She reached for her son's hand and pressed the velvet case into his palm.

Collin eyed it and her curiously. "What's this?"

"It's the engagement ring Jackson Broomes gave to me the day you were born. When we were first married, he couldn't afford a ring. He proposed with this gold band that he found at a pawnshop for twenty-five dollars." She pointed to a ring she was wearing on the pinkie of her right hand. "The day you were born, he proposed again and surprised me with this beauty."

Collin lifted the lid. Inside was a beautiful two-carat, princess-cut diamond, set in a simple white gold band.

"We ate beans for the next two years to pay off this ring. After your dad died and I was accepted at law school, I pawned it once or twice to feed us. But I always knew that one day I would give it to you. And that maybe you would want to give it to someone special. This one," she said, pointing a second time at the slim band around her pinkie, "has always felt like the hope and promise that we had when Jackson and I first fell in love, and the first time I ever took it off my ring finger was when I knew that Matthew was my future. This one, I hope to one day give to my granddaughter, since I never had a little girl."

Collin wrapped his arms around his mother's shoulders and hugged her tightly. He didn't miss the tears that misted her eyes. He kissed her cheek. "I love you, Mom."

Katrina kissed him back. "I love you, too. Now, go get some rest."

Collin headed toward the back door. He paused, his hand on the knob.

"Did you forget something?" his mom asked.

"No. I was wondering if you would help me with something?"

"Anything. You know that."

"Dad rented out the Cowboys Stadium to sweep you off your feet. Any ideas how I can top that?"

Two weeks after all charges were dismissed against Jerome James he was officially exonerated, his prison record purged. The court of inquiry ruled on Collin's petition, acknowledging there was probable cause to believe Victor Wells had violated criminal laws by concealing evidence. They formally charged him with criminal contempt. The State Bar of Texas also brought charges against him for ethical violations. Rumor had it he was trying to negotiate a plea deal, seeking reduced jail time in exchange for his resignation and the permanent surrender of his law license.

London had finally returned to her apartment, feeling better about everything. She and Collin had fallen into a comfortable routine with each other. Work was going well, the two moving on to separate cases with Perry's confidence in Collin's abilities at an all-time high. After a lengthy lecture, the director of operations had given their relationship his blessing. London's friends were ecstatic, teasing the two of them regularly. Weekends were spent between his family and hers, and they enjoyed serious quality time with each other. If it had been physically possible, they would have made love multiple times per day.

Collin had been surprised to discover her love for knitting and many an evening found her curled up on one end of the sofa with two needles and skeins of yarn in her lap. Almost always Collin sat on the other end, reading his book of the moment. Between the office, the law library, the courthouse and the ranch, they'd found balance, and it felt amazing.

After a particularly long day, Collin had gone to hang out with his father and brother, Jake playing basketball for a local youth league. London had stopped at the supermarket to buy everything she needed to make her mother's famous cheesecake. She was determined to surprise Collin with a late-night snack after he'd snacked on her. She had just pulled the grocery bags out of the trunk of her car, turning toward the apartment's entrance, when she saw him.

Victor Wells stood at the other end of the parking lot, staring. His expression was hard and menacing. He held a black police baton in one hand, slapping it against his other palm, the gesture threatening. London quickly swept the entirety of the parking lot with her eyes, praying that someone else was there and would see. A man parked midway between them was exiting his own car. She didn't recognize the stranger but was instantly grateful that someone stood in the way of Victor getting to her before she could get inside to safety. When she turned her attention back, Victor was sliding into the seat of his Cadillac. He eased his car out of the parking space, pulling past the man and then her. As he passed, he pointed the baton in her direction and laughed.

She was still shaking as she rushed to the door of her building. The other man caught up with her at the entrance.

"Do you need a hand with your bags?" he asked politely as he entered the door code, pulling it open to let them enter.

London shook her head. "No, thank you," she responded, throwing one last glance over her shoulder.

The stranger nodded. "Are you okay, miss?"

She eyed him cautiously, her expression reserved. "I'm fine."

The man nodded, moving to the mailboxes as she hurried to the elevator. As the conveyor doors closed behind her, the stranger was still staring, and London's fears increased tenfold.

Even after double- and then triple-checking the locks on her front door, London was still shaking. She looked out of her living room window down to the parking lot, searching out that Cadillac. Once she was certain the car, and Wells, were gone, her tears fell, saline cascading from her eyes like water from a busted pipe.

She cried and then, just like that, London got angry. Angrier than she could ever remember being. She'd been riding high on clouds of pure joy since Collin had come into her life. Things had turned around and she'd begun to trust her heart again. She'd finally begun to believe that she didn't have to be alone to be happy. She'd been grateful to let the past go, and now Victor was trying to steal her joy. The more she thought about him, the angrier she became. So much so that when Collin came through the door she was fuming with rage.

"That bastard was waiting for me in the parking lot," she snapped as he secured the entrance lock behind himself. She was pacing the floor, unable to contain the resentment spewing through her spirit. "He tried to intimidate me," she snapped. "And I almost let him get away with it! But I'm not going to let him hurt me. Not ever again."

Collin leaned back against the kitchen counter, his arms crossed. He listened as she ranted. Between the ranting and raving she told him about Victor and the strange man and their encounter in the parking lot. He let her rage until she was exhausted. Until she finally fell into his arms, allowing the weight of everything that had haunted her to finally fall away. He held her tightly, shouldering the last of whatever burdened her.

"You must think I'm crazy!" she exclaimed.

Collin shook his head. "No, I don't. I think I should have been here. I'm so sorry I couldn't get here sooner."

"We shouldn't have to live this way. I shouldn't be afraid to be alone."

"No, you shouldn't. I agree."

London stepped out of his arms. She moved back to the living room and the groceries she'd dropped in the center of the floor. Moving back to the kitchen,

she placed the bags on the counter and began to unpack the food. It was then that she realized the time.

"You're home early. I wasn't expecting you until
much later. I thought you planned to eat dinner with
Jake and your dad?"

Collin leaned across the center island, his hands
clasped together as he watched her. "My aunt Vanessa called and told me what happened. She didn't
know if you would call and tell me and she thought
you might need me."

"Your aunt? How did she…"

Collin smiled. "That strange man is part of the security detail she put on us. He's been watching after
you since the trial."

"Security?"

"I told you my family will do whatever is necessary to protect each other."

London nodded, the tears beginning to puddle behind
her eyelids a second time. She swiped a hand across her
face. "I was going to make you a cake," she said finally.

Collin chuckled, moving to where she stood and
wrapping his arms around her a second time. "You
are all the cake I will ever need!"

It was only a few days later when a truckload of
flowers was delivered, the deliveryman ringing the
bell for access. Collin had already left for court when
London met the driver on the steps into the building
and refused the delivery.

"What am I supposed to do with them?" the man
asked, throwing his hands up in frustration. "I can't
take them back!"

"I really don't care what you do with them," she

said as she stood with her hands on her hips, appraising the massive arrangements that filled the back of a U-Haul truck. "Is there a card?" she asked.

The man huffed as he pulled an envelope from a clipboard. London slid her finger beneath the flap and broke the seal. She pulled the notecard from inside and read it. "For your grave." The harsh words struck a nerve and she could feel her anger rising with a vengeance. The driver pulled her from her thoughts.

"Lady, I need to make this delivery. Someone needs to take these flowers."

"Someone will," she said. She reached for his clipboard and pen, jotting down an address and name. "Take them to the Genesis Women's Center. Here's their address and I'll call and tell them you're coming."

"And who do I say they're from?"

"If they ask, tell them the London Jacobs Domestic Violence Relief Fund sent them to brighten up the residential spaces."

The man shook his head, still feeling uncertain.

"Is there a problem?" London asked.

"Nah! It's whatever," he finally said as he hopped back into his vehicle and sped off.

The London Jacobs Domestic Violence Relief Fund. Until she'd spoken the words out loud it had only been an idea in the back of her mind. For too long, London had remained silent, too embarrassed and ashamed to speak about the trauma that had stolen such a huge chunk of her life. She wasn't interested in being silent one minute longer. She'd made the decision to stand in her truth and tell her story, to be a voice of hope and reason for other women going through the pain and shame she'd experienced. To maybe help one woman change her circumstances. She had a vision and goals and she was determined to see them through to fruition.

She headed toward her car. Once inside, she texted a message to Collin, asking him to meet her for lunch when he was finished. When he responded almost immediately, she smiled, started the engine and pulled out into traffic. In all of her excitement she didn't notice the three cars that pulled into traffic after her, following closely behind.

London was practically skipping as she completed her phone call with Barbara Jo at Genesis. The Dallas women's shelter and support facility was near and dear to her heart. They existed to give women and children in abusive situations a path to lead an independent and safe life. She had the utmost respect for what they were able to accomplish for families in need and it was one of her missions to be of service to them in any way she could. She had hoped the flowers would offer a little hope and joy and not the fear that had been intended.

So stoked, and riding a cloud of joy, London wasn't paying any attention when she stepped out of her car. She'd found a parking spot in the rear lot behind the restaurant and had been sitting in her vehicle for a good few minutes. Glancing quickly at her watch she realized Collin would soon be arriving if he hadn't already beat her there. She had just stepped out of the car to head inside when Victor suddenly stepped in behind her.

He grabbed her by the arm and spun her around,

slamming her hard against the side of her car. Shock and pain snatched the air from her lungs, her eyes widening in surprise.

"You really should have listened to me," Victor mused, his sinister expression marked by a demonic smile and a glazed stare.

London tried to scream but he held his forearm across her throat, leaning his full weight against her. She couldn't breathe, and her arms flailed as she struggled to get him off. He had just reared back his fist to throw a punch when Collin snatched him off her, his own punch landing against the side of Victor's head. London spun around and leaned over the car's hood, coughing and gasping for air. The two men wrestled like two bulls. They scuffled like prize-fighters, throwing punch for punch. It was chaos and madness. A crowd had begun to gather, cell phones held high to record everything. In the distance, London could hear sirens and then three men rushed in to pull Collin and Victor apart. She recognized the stranger who'd offered her help the other day and she realized the security team had not been far behind the two of them.

Victor's nose was bleeding and his eye had begun to swell. A large man had him down on the ground, his knee in Victor's back as he handcuffed his hands behind him. Collin and London were suddenly like long-lost lovers in a B-grade movie, screaming each other's name as they threw themselves against each other.

"London!"

"Collin!"

"Baby, are you okay?" Collin cupped his hands

around her face, kissing her forehead, her eyes, the tip of her nose. His fingers grazed the rising bruises around her neck.

She nodded as she pressed her hands against his chest, tears streaming from her eyes.

Vanessa suddenly appeared at their elbows. Collin wasn't surprised, grateful to see a familiar face. She barked orders at her people, her tone commanding.

"I need everything you have. Video, audio, all of it! Collin, you are going to have to go downtown," she said, pointing at the officers heading in their direction. "They will probably threaten you with an assault charge. I've already called your dad. He'll meet you there."

"You called my father?"

Vanessa grinned. "Baby, you know I keep my legal team on speed dial!"

Collin shook his head. Vanessa pointed him toward a police officer. He leaned to kiss London's lips. "It's going to be okay," he said. "Just do whatever Aunt Vanessa says."

London watched as Collin stepped toward the officers. They stood in conversation and before she knew it he was standing in handcuffs, being led to a police car.

"Why are they arresting him?" London cried.

Vanessa pressed a palm against London's back. "Baby girl, you need to give them your statement and then you need to go to the hospital. I'll ride with you. We need to make sure all of your bruises are entered into the record. And this is where it's going to get interesting. You are just days from the statute of limitations expiring on your last assault, the one that put you in the hospital and almost killed you. If you want this to end, you need to press charges on that assault *and* this one. You're going to need to remember everything you can about what happened back then."

London's voice was low. "You know about that?"

"Baby girl, I make it my business to know everything I can about the people I work for, to make sure I can be the best kind of support they need."

London took a deep breath. She took a step back and then moved around to the back of her car, popping the trunk open. Inside was a clear plastic tub with a red plastic lid. Inside the tub lay a number of file folders, each meticulously labeled. She lifted the container and passed it to Vanessa.

"The police reports, medical files, photographs and my personal journals detailing the abuse."

Vanessa's eyes widened. "You've been keeping all of this?"

London nodded. "I wanted to press charges. I was just too scared. I knew how manipulative and dishonest he could be and I knew he'd leverage everything in his arsenal against me. I kept all this so there would be proof when he called me a liar."

"Good girl!"

An officer interrupted them, demanding to know what had happened. Vanessa passed him her card, identifying herself.

"This young woman is London Jacobs. Ms. Jacobs was assaulted by Victor Wells. He's been stalking her for years. For the past few weeks my security team has had Ms. Jacobs under protective surveillance and we've captured Wells on video stalking and threatening her. Her boyfriend, Attorney Collin Stallion, arrived a few minutes ago and witnessed Mr. Wells assaulting her. He pulled the man off her and acted in self-defense."

"Is that what happened, miss?" the officer asked.

"Yes. Victor Wells has assaulted me on previous occasions, as well. My boyfriend was only trying to help me."

"Did you press charges against this Wells guy?"

London shook her head. "No, I didn't."

Before the officer could ask anything else, Vanessa waved over the EMT person. "Ms. Jacobs needs to go to the hospital. Can this wait?"

"I'm sure we'll have more questions," the officer stated.

"That's fine. Ms. Jacobs will be more than willing to answer them.

When Collin walked out of the police station, his father following closely on his heels, his mother was standing in the lobby, waiting for them. She stood with her arms crossed, one high-heeled foot tapping at the concrete floor. Relief washed over her expression when she saw them.

"What happened?" she asked, kissing her son and then her husband.

Matthew smiled. "They're not going to press charges against Collin. In fact, I think someone actually said our son was a hero."

Katrina rolled her eyes. She looped her arm through her husband's. "This is the second time you've had to get my wayward son out of trouble, Mr. Stallion. I'm going to have to show you my appreciation."

Matthew leaned to kiss her lips. "Yes, please!"

"Ewww!" Collin said, grinning broadly. "Too much information!"

His parents laughed.

"What about Justice Wells? What's going to happen with him?" Katrina asked. They descended the steps and were headed in the direction of the parking lot.

"I'm told he'll be indicted in the morning. They have eyewitness testimony and video to confirm everything Collin and London said about what happened. Also, because of all the evidence Vanessa has about his history and the prior violence against London, they're going to charge him with attempted murder. The prosecutor is going to request he get no bail. I don't think we'll have to worry about Victor Wells ever again."

"Thank goodness!" Katrina exclaimed.

"I plan to do whatever it takes to make sure he can't ever hurt London ever again," Collin stated.

Matthew slapped his son against his back. "I'm glad everything ended well. You and London had us worried for a minute."

"Aunt Vanessa was probably just a bit dramatic when she called. I had everything under control."

"Was that before you threw your first punch at Wells or after?"

"That son of a bitch had London by the throat! He should be glad all I did was throw a punch!" Collin shook his head. "I need to find London. I need to make sure she's okay."

"She's still at the hospital," Katrina noted. "They just wanted to run some tests before they released her. And watch your mouth, please! You still are not that grown to be cussing around me," she admonished.

Collin kissed her cheek and shook his father's hand. "Thank you," he said, meeting his father's stare evenly. "I truly appreciate you both."

"You know we're always here if you need us," Matthew said.

Collin smiled. "Yes, sir. And I trust it with every fiber of my being."

When London was finally released from the hospital, the doctor sending her home with prescriptions for pain pills, a muscle relaxant and a sedative to help her sleep, Collin was right there to take her home.

He held her hand as they exited the medical center, helping her to his car. When she was seated comfortably in the passenger seat of his new Mercedes, he paused, leaning to kiss her cheek and squeeze her hand.

"Are you sure you're okay?" he asked.

London smiled. "I'm really good. I just want to go home. I want to crawl into bed and fall asleep dreaming about you."

Collin grinned. "A Stallion dream, huh?"

"The best kind!"

As he maneuvered the car toward her apartment, he gave her a quick update, telling her what had happened at the station and what they knew about the charges that would be pressed against Victor Wells.

"Let's not talk about him anymore. We have better things to focus on. I have a dream, too, and I'm hoping you'll want to be a part of it," she said.

As he drove, he listened, London giving him an update on her intentions and the new business she envisioned. When she finished, she looked anxiously toward him for his opinion.

"I think it's a brilliant idea," he finally said, "but it's going to have to wait until we get back."

"Get back? From where?"

"Spain."

"We're going to Spain?"

"Yes. We're flying to Spain on a private jet. We'll spend a week acting like tourists and at some point during our trip, I'm going to ask you to be my wife."

"Your wife?"

"Mrs. Collin Stallion! The first, the last and the only." He shot her a quick look. "You good with that?"

London grinned. "For now!" And then she kissed him, every one of her Stallion dreams having come true!

* * * * *

COMING NEXT MONTH
Available September 18, 2018

#589 SEDUCTIVE MEMORY
Moonlight and Passion • **by AlTonya Washington**
A chance encounter with Paula Starker is all entrepreneur Linus Brooks needs to try to win back the sultry Philadelphia DA. And where better to romance her than on a tropical island? But before they can share a future, Linus will have to reveal his tragic secret…

#590 A LOS ANGELES PASSION
Millionaire Moguls • **by Sherelle Green**
Award-winning screenwriter Trey Moore agrees to look after his infant nephew for two weeks. Gorgeous Kiara Woods, owner of LA's glitziest day care, offers to help. While she's teaching Trey babysitting 101, she's falling hard for the millionaire. But can she risk revealing a painful truth that's already cost her so much?

#591 HER PERFECT PLEASURE
Miami Strong • **by Lindsay Evans**
Lawyer and businessman Carter Diallo solves problems for his powerful family's corporation. But when his influential powers fail him, the Diallos bring in PR wizard—and Carter's *ex-lover*—Jade Tremaine. Ten years ago, Carter left Jade emotionally devastated. Now the guy known as The Magic Man must win back Jade's trust…

#592 TEMPTING THE BILLIONAIRE
Passion Grove • **by Niobia Bryant**
Betrayed by his fiancée, self-made billionaire Chance Castillo plans to sue his ex for her share of their million-dollar wedding. His unexpected attraction to his new attorney takes his mind off his troubles. But Ngozi Johns *never* dates a client. Until one steamy night with the gorgeous Dominican changes *everything*.

Get 4 FREE REWARDS!

We'll send you 2 FREE Books plus 2 FREE Mystery Gifts.

Harlequin® Desire books feature heroes who have it all: wealth, status, incredible good looks... everything but the right woman.

FREE
Value Over
$20

SPECIAL EXCERPT FROM

HARLEQUIN®

Award-winning screenwriter Trey Moore agrees to look after his infant nephew for two weeks, and for once he's out of his depth. Gorgeous Kiara Woods, owner of LA's glitziest day care, offers help. While she's teaching Trey Babysitting 101, she's falling hard for the sexy millionaire. But can she risk revealing a painful truth that's already cost her so much?

Read on for a sneak peek at
A Los Angeles Passion/
the next exciting installment in the
Millionaire Moguls continuity by Sherelle Green!

"I had a nice time tonight," Kiara said when she reached the door. When she didn't hear a response, she turned around to find him watching her intently.

"I had a nice time, as well." Trey took a step closer to her. "I enjoyed getting to know you a little better." He was so close, Kiara was afraid to breathe.

"Me, too," she whispered. His eyes dropped to her lips and stayed there for a while. After a few moments, she forced herself to swallow the lump in her throat.

He took another step closer, so she took another step back, only to be met with the door. When his hand reached up to cup her face, Kiara completely froze. *There's no way he's going to kiss me, right? We just met each other.*

"Do you want me to stop?" he asked.

Say yes. Say yes. Say yes. "No," she said, moments before his lips came crashing down onto hers. Her hands flew to the back of his neck as he gently pushed her against the door. Kiara had experienced plenty

KPEXP0918

of first kisses in the past, but this was unlike any first kiss she'd ever had. Trey's lips were soft, yet demanding. Eager, yet controlled. When she parted her lips to get a better taste, his tongue briefly swooped into her mouth before he ended their kiss with a soft peck and backed away.

Kiara couldn't be sure how she looked, but she certainly felt unhinged and downright aroused.

"Come on," Trey said with a nod. "I'll walk you to your car."

How is he even functioning after that kiss? Kiara felt like she glided to the car, rather than walked. Yet Trey looked as composed as ever.

"We should get together again soon," Trey said, opening her car door. Kiara sat down in the driver's seat and looked up at Trey. He flashed her a sexy smile.

"And for the record, this was definitely a date," Trey said with a wink. "I didn't stop kissing you because I wasn't enjoying it, nor was I trying to tease you. I stopped kissing you because if I hadn't, I'd be ready to drag you into my bedroom. Which also brings me to the reason I didn't show you my bedroom. I didn't trust myself not to make a move." Trey leaned a little closer. "When we make love, I want us to know one another a little better, so I forced myself to stop kissing you tonight and it was damn hard to do so. Have a good night, Kiara."

Trey softly kissed her cheek and closed her door before she could vocalize a response. Quite frankly, she didn't think she had anything to say anyway. Her mind was still reeling and her lips were still tingling from that explosive kiss.

Kiara gave a quick wave. *I told you not to get out of the car earlier*, that voice in her head teased. She started her car and drove away from Trey's house.

"What the hell just happened?" She'd originally thought that she could avoid him or keep their relationship strictly friendly. Now she wasn't so sure. Kissing Trey had awakened desires she thought she'd long buried. Feelings she'd ignored and pushed aside.

Kiara made it to her home a few minutes later. She glanced at her house before dropping her head to the steering wheel. She was in deep and she knew it. To make matters worse, she only lived a five-minute drive from Trey's house, meaning there was no way she was getting any sleep tonight knowing a man that sexy was only a couple miles away.

Don't miss A Los Angeles Passion
by Sherelle Green, available October 2018
wherever Harlequin® Kimani Romance™
books and ebooks are sold.

Want to give in to temptation with
steamy tales of irresistible desire?

Check out **Harlequin® Presents®,
Harlequin® Desire** and
Harlequin® Kimani™ Romance books!

New books available every month!

CONNECT WITH US AT:

Facebook.com/groups/HarlequinConnection

 Facebook.com/HarlequinBooks

Twitter.com/HarlequinBooks

 Instagram.com/HarlequinBooks

Pinterest.com/HarlequinBooks

ReaderService.com

 **HARLEQUIN®**

**ROMANCE WHEN
YOU NEED IT**

PGENRE2018

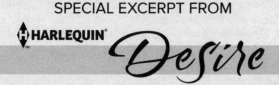
Benjamin Bennett was a catch by anyone's standards—
even before you factored in his healthy bank account.
But he was her best friend's little brother. And though he
was all grown-up now, he was just a kid compared to her.

Flirting with Benji would start tongues wagging all
over Magnolia Lake. Not that she cared what they thought
of her. But if the whole town started talking, it would
make things uncomfortable for the people she loved.

"Thanks for the dance."

Benji lowered their joined hands but didn't let go.
Instead, he leaned down, his lips brushing her ear and his
well-trimmed beard gently scraping her neck. "Let's get
out of here."

It was a bad idea. A really bad idea.

Her cheeks burned. "But it's your cousin's wedding."

He nodded toward Blake, who was dancing with his

bride, Savannah, as their infant son slept on his shoulder. The man was in complete bliss.

"I doubt he'll notice I'm gone. Besides, you'd be rescuing me. If Jeb Dawson tells me one more time about his latest invention—"

"Okay, okay." Sloane held back a giggle as she glanced around the room. "You need to escape as badly as I do. But there's no way we're leaving here together. It'd be on the front page of the newspaper by morning."

"Valid point." Benji chuckled. "So meet me at the cabin."

"The cabin on the lake?" She had so many great memories of weekends spent there.

It would just be two old friends catching up on each other's lives. Nothing wrong with that.

She repeated it three times in her head. But there was nothing friendly about the sensations that danced along her spine when he'd held her in his arms and pinned her with that piercing gaze.

"Okay. Maybe we can catch up over a cup of coffee or something."

"Or something." The corner of his sensuous mouth curved in a smirk.

A shiver ran through her as she wondered, for the briefest moment, how his lips would taste.

Don't miss
The Billionaire's Legacy *by Reese Ryan,*
part of the Billionaires and Babies series!

Available October 2018 wherever
Harlequin® Desire books and ebooks are sold.

www.Harlequin.com